CW00569116

SECRET LIFE OF DATA
ANTHOLOGY

UK Research
and Innovation

BRISTOL BOOKS

Bristol Books CIC, The Courtyard, Wraxall,
Wraxall Hill, Bristol, BS48 1NA

Secret Life of Data Anthology

Published by Bristol Books 2022

ISBN: 978-1-909446-35-9

Typesetting and cover design: Joe Burt

Copyright: University of Bristol/Individual Contributors/Bristol Books
All rights reserved

University of Bristol and the individual contributors have asserted their right under the Copyright, Designs and Patents Act of 1988 to be identified as the authors of this work. This book may not be reproduced or transmitted in any form or by any means without the prior written consent of the publisher, except by a reviewer who wishes to quote passages in connection with a review written in a newspaper or magazine or broadcast on television, radio or on the internet.

A CIP record of this book is available at the British Library.

Printed using paper from a sustainable source.

MIX
Paper from
responsible sources
FSC® C020438

WORLD
LAND
TRUST™

www.carbonbalancedprint.com
CBP2250

INTRODUCTION

By Genevieve Liveley & Lizzie Coles-Kemp

"We're an information economy. They teach you that in school. What they don't tell you is that it's impossible to move, to live, to operate at any level without leaving traces, bits, seemingly meaningless fragments of personal information. Fragments that can be retrieved, amplified..."

— WILLIAM GIBSON, JOHNNY MNEMONIC

When we think about the security of data on our phones and computers, we might think about passwords and permissions, or about data encryption – but we rarely think about what our data looks like, or what it does as it moves around hidden inside our phones, computers, digital devices, our apps and networks. This *secret life of data* – the traces, bits, and fragments of personal information that we leave behind us online – is the focus of this short story collection.

Funded through the ESRC's Digital Security by Design (Discribe) Hub+, the collection draws together the ten best creative stories submitted in response to a competition coordinated by the Jean Golding Institute in the summer of 2022. Creative writers worldwide were invited to tell stories that would animate the *secret life of data* – perhaps imagining this life as a journey, a quest, a romance, or a tragedy; thinking of a computer's internal architecture as a house, a jungle, a zoo, or a city; and the data as characters facing danger in the form of various digital threats and vulnerabilities.

Discribe Hub+ is a research initiative that explores the social and cultural factors that might influence future successes in computer chip design. The competition and this resulting collection of stories form part of Discribe Hub+'s Futures Programme. This focuses on innovative ways to explore what it can mean socially and culturally for digital technologies to be secure by design. This anthology of short stories will help research communities, policy makers, and technologists think more creatively about the movement of data through the new computer chip architectures that will form the cornerstone of a digital security by design approach.

The original short stories collected in this anthology offer keen insights into the digital world – past, present, and future – through metaphor and analogy. They imaginatively animate the ways our data interacts with computer software and hardware, exploring how it can be threatened and protected. They reflect upon what one author describes as 'the politics of data' and the myriad ways in which data itself can be used to 'tell different stories.' They use similes to open up new ways of thinking about data and digital technologies. In one of the stories anthologised here, a character describes 'the inside of a computer being like a wedding ... the marriage of data and processing that gets showered with confetti ... scraps of algorithms and short chains of code'.

Some of the narratives offer a darkly dystopian vision of our digital futures, but many find space for optimism. One imagines a future in which software engineering becomes one of the most highly regulated professions: 'Where once you could go from rookie to pushing to production after a 12-week boot camp, now a degree in computer science took longer to obtain than one in medicine.'

Others take a light-hearted approach, imagining the secret life of data as akin to the organic subterranean life of our gardens, or to the dynamics of a fairytale royal court. One story imagines the inner space of a computer as a seedy bar where dangers lurk in every corner ('... are those files corrupting over there?'), others picture it as an archaeological site or a hospital ward.

Analogy and metaphor provide the ideal vehicles for anticipatory imagining and futures thinking in this context. Indeed, research in science and technology studies, futures studies, and cognate disciplines, highlights the importance of analogy, simile, and metaphor as the basic building-blocks that we need for the production of new scientific knowledge. Analogies build the foundations for innovation and help drive change to legacy systems – to business as usual – by allowing communities to think about and talk about an emerging technical phenomenon in familiar terms, as something already part of the fabric of the world they know, as a novel introduction not into a vacuum but into a pre-existing world.

Analogy is how we imagine and make sense of new and complex concepts. And such creative imaginings are especially useful to the research of the DiScriBe Hub+ because they help to generate new insights into the possibilities involved in the adoption of new secure technologies in the context of a volatile, uncertain, complex, and ambiguous future.

The DiScriBe Hub+ Futures Programme has already used a variety of creative engagement techniques grounded in the arts and humanities to bring together different stakeholder groups using novel methods for understanding the future potential of Digital Security by Design. The stories in this collection all offer fresh 'data' to help create a richer description of the possible futures the technical community imagines for the next generation of security hardware technologies. We hope you enjoy them!

Genevieve Liveley and Lizzie Coles-Kemp

CATNAP

Ola Michalec

1.

The heatwave has entered its fourth day. Days stretch lazily in what appears to be a 96-hour long collective doze. At the record-breaking 42 degrees, air particles start to tremble, creating a mirage of imaginary planes and balloons. Looking out of the window, I noticed a group of builders working on a roof extension with their radio on.

They were joined in unison singing along to Ella Fitzgerald's "Dream a little dream of me" – huh, a strange choice for a group of brawny, young men.

I have decided to work from home, partly to avoid human contact, partly to finish my analysis before the next week's deadline. I should really be writing an important breakthrough paper – a novel theory of our digital society. The problem is, I simply have nothing to write. Despite being paid to think, I have become deeply convinced all that's to theorise about digital technologies has already been written. Therefore, I have taken refuge in the safe but undeniably bland world of literature reviews. The prospect of going through dozens of past papers on digital surveillance doesn't fill me with joy. Sorting through the pile labelled "theory", I watch as the minute hand of the clock crawls towards the upward position, marking four in the afternoon. Was it Dencik who wrote about data justice or Zuboff? What did Nissenbaum really mean when coining the term "contextual privacy"? Do we have enough pasta for dinner tonight? It has now become apparent that I am looking for any excuse to look away from my laptop.

Procrastination is easy when you have a furry companion. I am very lucky to be a friend of Toggles, a former street cat who moved into my apartment one morning about five years ago. No one really knows her origin story or even her life before we met. I can only presume she had been dealing with some unsavoury characters in the past, as she used to be quite fickle. One second, she'd be asking for affection, next – she'd do a one-eighty, running around the house hissing and growling.

Times have changed since then and so has Toggles. Her current routines are absolutely enthralling, worthy of her own YouTube channel. Take her morning habits. Every day, she wakes me up minutes before the sunrise, as if she insisted I appreciated the beauty of nature with her. When I fail to do so (it's 5am, Toggles!), she traverses my half-awake body so I toss and turn enough to make space for her on the bed. Inevitably, when I wake up, I find Toggles taking no less than three quarters of the bed. Toggles won't let me get up unless I pet her. How could my boss expect me to be at my desk at 9am when this tortoiseshell pancake is peacefully snoring on my head?

Sometimes Toggles disappears for hours. One minute she moves through the hedge in the back garden, next – she's gone. Where does she go? Who does she meet? What is she up to? I once read a paper (*"Applying the Global Positioning System to investigate ranging characteristics of the of Felis catus in an urban environment"*) where researchers installed GPS trackers to cats' collars to find out the answer to exactly these questions. It turned out that on average, city cats don't roam further than 500 meters. Hard to believe given the long hours she's enjoying away from home! In the spirit of reproducible science, I have decided to spend the rest of the afternoon replicating the experiment.

For an extra £2 charge, I could purchase a GPS tracker and a camera using Amazons' new feature of hyper-eco-express 1 hour delivery. With all profits going towards delivery drivers' wages and Amazon's fleet being fully electrified, I almost feel virtuous about purchasing goods from a big tech corporation. Perhaps the feature comes with pages of fine print in T&C's but I don't really have time to read all that. After a speedy postage and ceremonial unboxing (I had to record this event for my semi-professional Twitter account), I equip Toggles with a GPS tracker and a camera I could now see the world from a feline perspective, thanks to the mass-produced cheap electronics, and integration with a clever app called Cat Eye. We truly live in the IoT times. The Internet of Toggles' era has begun!

I've attached the tracker and the camera around her collar. Taken together, they weigh no more than a standard bell. I've remarked on that, as if I wanted to justify spying on my own cat. Ironic, one might say, for a surveillance researcher to spy on her own cat. Isn't this the ultimate display of human dominance over animals?

What's a feline theory of privacy, anyway? I battle against a strong feeling of discomfort that in the end turned out to be no stronger than my sense of curiosity.

Besides, Toggles doesn't seem to mind – she just ruffles her whiskers and stretches her paws out in a long arching motion. Anyway, I hope that whoever said "curiosity killed the cat" didn't mean it literally.

Following the successful installation of the device, I now have to integrate it with Cat Eye software. As far as surveillance capitalism goes, Cat Eye boasts an interesting business model. Cat Eye is a free open-source app, developed by a charity – with all profits being redirected towards animal shelters. They make money from displaying highly personalised adverts to their users, for which they need permissions to various phone data – from contacts, photos, to browsing history and location. Given how much information I gave them, it's strange how they still manage to get personalisation so wrong. For example, they incorrectly inferred my cat has lost weight by analysing a series of photos taken over the past few years. I have kindly received some recommendations for "fattening" cat food: "we have estimated that Toggles' chonk index is 20% below the average for a healthy adult cat. Have you considered purchasing Paw's Delight Premium feline nutritional complex, available in pouches, cans and biscuits? We're offering 20% off for orders placed before midnight – hurry!". This is going to amuse my vet who called Toggles "Rubenesque" during the last visit.

After tinkering with app settings and privacy permissions (yet again, I had to give away lots of personal data to access the best video resolution – I swear, this is the first and only time!), I launch the app to see Toggles' location on the map and a live recording of her adventures. Oh, she's leaving the back garden through a hole in the hedge, as usual. I bet she'll end up on the Turners' deckchairs; a well-known afternoon suntrap.

BZZZZ...FZZZZ...TZZZZ... – what used to be a sharp video of my hedge has pixelated to a snow-screen emitting unbearable white noise. Looks like the camera is bricked already. Typical IoT – not only it harvests all your personal data but also breaks after the first use. Well, before the first use, in my case. If this isn't a clear sign to get back to work, then I don't know what would be.

I return to my desk to continue reviewing the literature. I was making my way through a classic page-turner entitled "A taxonomy of privacy" (Solove, 2006, for those of you who'd like to follow up). A sharp but bright 8-bit windows jingle disrupts my flow. I switched my attention back to the camera feed which appears to be showing the animations from Windows Media Player circa '99. Looks like Cat Eye's developers are nostalgic for the golden era of the internet. I could have easily dismissed this event as a bug in the system, but then I noticed Toggles' paws resolutely moving forward, barely captured with the edge of the camera. Perhaps she is going to show me her secret hideout after all?

2.

I keep my gaze on the footage, hoping that it will provide me with some answers. A few swirly Y2K visuals later, I find myself staring at a very modern control room – complete with several large screens, busy analysts and a flashing array of red buttons implying important decisions. Usually, a control room would manage the movement of trains or supply of electricity. Judging from the fast-paced noisy exchanges between the analysts, this place was responsible for something else, namely the Recommender Algorithm. The Algorithm is responsible for curating content across all social media as we know it. Each screen displayed a different Internet celebrity cat: a Nyan Cat, a Grumpy Cat, Bilbo Cat, Yass Cat, Keyboard Cat and Jorts. In the centre of the room, a massive live infographic displayed numbers of followers, user engagement and recent comments from people watching cat-themed videos. Oh, perhaps it's worth mentioning that all analysts in the room are cats.

Although at this stage it shouldn't come as a surprise.

I follow Toggles to the boardroom where a group of felines with iced latte bowls and curled 'hipster' whiskers (you couldn't make it up!) are pitching ideas for the next TikTok sensation to their bosses. From their quick exchange, I gather that the men, I mean, the cats running the show are Jeff Tailzos and Elon Meowsk. Apparently, the next internet celebrity will be a boisterous and very entrepreneurial cat "employed" in a pizzeria as a Chief Dough Kneader, with all sanitary precautions, obviously. Bosses love it, purring loudly to express their approval. Fascinating how their society mirrors ours.

After a short lunch break (although I certainly do not approve of the idea of Dreamies as a nutritious meal), the camera turns to another computer. Toggles is switching a machine on and loading a file. She then proceeds to give a presentation to her bosses. Toggles figured out that she needs to meow at minimum 70db to attract a human's attention before mealtimes, otherwise the human is too engrossed in her social media... the extent of animal neglect nowadays! Wait, *I* am the human she was talking about! All this time my tiny, fluffy cat has been watching me. All this time, I have been too busy looking at pixel cats to take care of the one made of flesh and bones.

3.

"I'm so sorry, my dear. Oh, how I'd love to be able to make it up to you!" – I whispered to myself, irrationally hoping that the cat might somehow hear me through her connected devices. Indeed, the only logical way to repair the damage would be to delete my social media accounts and turn attention to Toggles. Alas, we were quite literally in different dimensions. It's almost as if Toggles can sense my discomfort, as she roams around the control room and begins telling a story, monologuing into the void of imaginary listeners:

"Humans have been obsessed with us for a very long time. Starting from ancient Egypt, five thousand years ago, we were already considered magical and godlike back then. Every village in the Nile delta erected a statue for us. We had learnt some tricks to gain our status. We made sure to be visible during important events; the birth of a Pharoah's son, harvest celebration or New Year's festivities. Humans quickly concluded that we were the ones bringing good fortunes. This relationship worked well for a few thousand years until Pharaoh Nectanebo II introduced a dog as a new companion for his servants. This did not go down well with my ancestors, to say the least. Let me tell you, it was not the Romans who ultimately brought about the collapse of the Egyptian civilisation.

Over centuries, feline prowess grew only stronger. Recall all of those times wondering why cats sleep so much? We rarely sleep: we observe, record and learn. In accompanying people as domestic animals, we learnt languages, maths, musical instruments, and more recently – programming. And since history likes to repeat itself, we can draw some parallels between the ancient Egypt and modern times.

Early 1990s saw an explosion of digital toys – talking dolls, Furbies, Tamagotchi. The Daily Reporter once announced on their cover page "500% rise in Tamagotchi sales – pets are soon to become redundant". But we would not be so easily forgotten. This is why we came up with the concept of Virality. We watched humans for hours to analyse what makes them laugh, then recorded some videos to appeal to their sense of humour (we started with the now legendary cat, Thomas, playing keyboard in 1992 – a barrel of laughter really!). Finally, we created lots of fake accounts to spread the film across chat rooms and mailing lists.

Over the next three decades, we have been optimising the Recommender Algorithm across all internet platforms so that humans would become obsessed with us, feeding us ever more gourmet meals and gifting us precious toys. We built a perfect world not only for our species but for theirs as well – humans revelled in online fora, making friends with fellow (what they called) "cat people". The internet burgeoned with pages sharing tonnes of advice on how to take care of your pets (all heavily edited by our content creators, of course). I don't mean to brag, but we are the most popular category of YouTube videos with over 26 billion views and counting.

Recently, however, things have got out of control. We have realised humans have been preoccupied with the *representations* of cats, rather than the real ones! Meanwhile, my brothers and sisters suffer from neglect and abandon. People spend all of their free time on social media, leaving behind chores and opportunities to bond with their loved ones. On average, a modern domestic cat receives 2 minutes of petting time per week, a dramatic decrease from the early 00s, let alone ancient Egypt. Our worst nightmare is in our bowls, however. These days, we rarely eat Whiskas or Purina. Instead, we're being fed with microwaved vegan (!) dinner leftovers. Deprived of attention, our souls and bodies get sick. We fight instead of playing, we retreat instead of lounging" – Toggles managed to wrap her impassioned speech as her voice was about to crack.

The atmosphere in the room is tense.

"Optimising for 'high engagement' on social media doesn't work anymore. We have turned our humans into zombies" – Elon Meowsk concluded – "we now must take drastic action. What happened in the ancient Egypt wasn't an easy resolution, but it was necessary to keep our kin alive".

Toggles gasped.

"Bringing the balance of powers back to its natural state will require some collateral damage. Only one of them can survive: we can either spare the humanity or the internet," Jeff Tailzos added.

Toggles is coughing.

"Heckin' hairball! Excuse me, I'd rather sort it out in the bathroom."

Toggles runs to the toilet and grooms herself to calm down.

Suddenly, I become aware of my own reflection in the bathroom mirror. This could easily be a zoom call, except I was dialling across dimensions. How they managed to film me this whole time will remain a mystery to this day, although all I can say is that conspiracy nuts who covered their laptop camera with gaffer tape were right all along.

"Something serious is about to happen and it's your job, as a scholar, to write about it" – Toggles whispered.

"I have just gathered that from the chat with your boss, don't you worry. So, who are you going to get rid of then, us or data centres? Little observation: if we all die, I won't be able to write. I won't get much readership, either," I replied, somewhat sardonically.

"Apologies, Elon is all talk and no trousers. We will not inflict harm on anyone. For now, stay vigilant, observe, and write," she responded before leaping out through the window, leaving me alone in this strange virtual room.

4.

The next thing I remember is waking up with a headache on a sofa, cat peacefully snoozing on my lap. Her camera and GPS tracker smashed into pieces. Was it all a dream? It's 7pm already. I probably fell asleep out of heat exhaustion. I'd better drink some water and finish that analysis.

Despite my best efforts to focus on privacy taxonomies, I couldn't shake off a sense of queasiness. I decided to scroll down BBC News to bring myself back to the real world. A headline immediately captured my attention: "All images and videos featuring cats have been removed from the Internet". I kept reading: "In what appears to be a world-wide cyber-attack, unnamed hackers removed all images and videos of cats from the Internet replacing it with a message "May I have your attention?" Uncanny! I looked at Toggles, in search of an explanation. She purred happily half-asleep, without giving anything away.

Next few days were a whirlwind of reactions to this strange event. Everyone on Twitter turned into a cyber security expert, explaining possible motivations of the attackers. Police joined forces internationally, intending to capture the hacker – after all, whoever could access and delete all cat videos from the internet, should surely have powers to destroy more. A group of indie filmmakers decided that the most appropriate response is to start recording their Felixes and Lunas playing with strings or chasing toy mice. None of the above worked. The disappearance of cat images was beyond the current state of cyber security knowledge, the hackers did not feature in any criminal records and every new footage was automatically self-deleting. People around towns, villages and Facebook groups became progressively worried.

"Is this the end of the Internet as we know it?" some despaired.

"Are we at the brink of the first worldwide cyber war?" others proclaimed.

I glance at Toggles to see if she shares any of these concerns, but she is curled up in a ball in-between her favourite two jumpers, She is nothing but serene – after all, we spend a whole afternoon together watching local birds; our legs stretched across the sofa.

"Stay vigilant, observe, and write," a partially threatening, and a partially motivating banner flashed over my eyes as I was trying to connect to the work laptop. I have heard this phrase before. It might not be the usual motivational quote I'd place on my desk, but it made me realise that now I *do* have something to write. I cracked my knuckles and began to pour my thoughts onto the screen.

In a single sitting, I blasted an essay called "May I have your attention? Towards the anthropology of friendships in a post-digital age." My main argument is that tech debates miss a very important dimension. Scholars have predominantly focused on micro (individual) and macro (institutional) levels of analysis. By investigating issues like digital addiction on one side of the spectrum, and the powers of tech corporations and states, on the other, they ignore the relational level of analysis. Meanwhile, we need to better understand the qualities of relationships afforded by digital technologies. Most importantly, digital technologies which don't serve relationships should be rejected all together.

The essay immediately became popular, striking a chord with researchers and members of the public alike. Although it could be Elon Meowsk manipulating the Recommender Algorithm again. Eventually, people gave up on internet cats and returned to their real-life pets. The balance of powers got restored, one might say.

Human relationships changed as well. It has become a norm to turn off your phone ahead of socialising in order to fully focus on the interlocutor. Some public places, like cafes and train stations disabled network access on their premises so that strangers are encouraged to speak to one another. I am still struggling with the intensity of enduring eye contact during those mandatory conversations and often find myself instinctively reaching out for my phone that would have acted as a social anxiety shield in the past. Perhaps I should get over myself and accept we have entered a post-digital era, at my own request. At least pub quizzes are a fair game again.

Ola Michalec Ola is a social scientist based in the School of Computer Sciences at the University of Bristol. She researches 'the making of' computers that keep our world running, like the ones found in trains or power plants.

HARRASMENT

Alyson Hilbourne

"Is this seat taken?"

The question came from a quietly spoken man whom Veronica had never seen before. She looked up in surprise. The café wasn't crowded. There were plenty of other tables he could have chosen.

"Err … no … I suppose not."

Veronica glanced up at a face partially hidden by rimless bottle-bottom glasses of lapis blue. For an uncomfortable moment she thought they were eyes, huge and alien like, and suppressed a shudder.

The man was dressed in a blue Mao jacket that put Veronica in mind of drone-like workers and, as he lowered his cup to the table, she saw his fingernails were short and his fingers thick and wedge-like. A strong smell of fresh coffee wafted over from the black Americano.

Veronica went back to typing a message on her computer. A prickle at the back of her neck made her look up again. He was staring. He didn't appear to mind that he had been caught.

"Be careful with drinks near the computer."

He smiled at her.

Veronica frowned.

"I see lots of computers with coffee, coke or wine in the works. People think they're ruined, but not always. Often a hard drive can be viable. Bits of information get left behind for those prepared to look."

The man had a clipped way of talking. He didn't waste words, which made Veronica wonder why had he sat with her and begun to speak. All she wanted was a quiet coffee and to check on her Instagram. Why had some computer weirdo come to sit at her table? She was half inclined to gather her stuff together and move, but she really needed to send this message now it was half written. She glanced down at the list by her hand and transferred some figures to the email.

"Ever done that?"

"Eh, what?"

"Spilled a drink on a computer."

Veronica looked at him, her eyes narrowed slightly.

"Well, yes actually. I spilled water on the computer. It was very annoying. I lost a lot of stuff. I didn't have it backed up."

"So you did what?" he asked.

Veronica shrugged.

"I threw it out. It was no use ... wouldn't work."

"You need to be careful with old computers."

The light from the retro light bulbs that hung from pipes along the concrete ceiling of the coffee shop glinted off the man's glasses making them opaque and Veronica couldn't see his eyes. Man, he was creepy.

"I like to think of the inside of a computer being like a wedding," the man continued. "We have the marriage of data and processing that gets showered with confetti. The bits of confetti, scraps of algorithms and short chains of code, scatter all round the place — maybe not individually identifiable, but if someone is prepared to do the painstaking work and pick up all the bits they might work out who got married, how long ago, where they came from, and a lot more about them. Faint traces of the marriage remain hidden deep in the hard drive long after the wedding has been forgotten, like the paperwork left in a registry office. Then, if the bride happens to put down her bouquet and mislays it – leaves it on a windowsill and can't find it, or throws it to a bridesmaid, you'd think it was gone, wouldn't you. But that can be traced, too. Might be older, curling up at the edges even though, of course, that doesn't quite happen to data, but everything the bride touched can be traced, back to the flower shop or the bridal organizer who made it."

Veronica stared at the man, her eyes glazing slightly. She didn't entirely understand what he was talking about. She wondered if perhaps he was high on something.

"I sort through the bits," the man continued. "Seek out the hiding places, retrieve information as if it is confetti tucking into hidey holes behind the walls, buried in the grass or mud, in crevices and other dark places. Sometimes it's damaged, torn round the edges, damp or stained, but I massage the bits back to life, and pump them up until they give up secrets. It's not difficult. Many computers are not protected, and even then it's easy to break in. Once I have enough of the bits of confetti I can find a trail, seek out the type, the manufacturer, where it was bought, narrow it down until I find out whose wedding it was. When I have a name I search Instagram, TikTok, Twitter or Google or whatever. I can find date of birth, address, name of dog, or boyfriend. I can find out everything, eh, Veronica?"

Veronica sat up straight, her muscles taut and nerve endings jingling. He hadn't sat here by accident. He knew her name. She shifted in her seat. What did he want? Was he some sort of maniac?

Don't be silly.

Veronica tried to calm her breathing. He must have overheard someone calling her. Maybe he had been following her. No! Did he know where she lived? The inside of her mouth was dry and she felt hot as she thought about the number of times she'd been alone in the last few days. She looked around to check there were still customers in the cafe. People were talking and music was playing in the background, but Veronica had tuned them out like interfering static.

The man continued to stare at her, through his eyeless glasses. He lifted a hand from the table and reached down into the pocket of his jacket.

Veronica gasped. What was he getting out?

A gun, a knife?

She shuddered.

What if he wouldn't let her leave? Would she be able to alert somebody? She looked wildly about at the other customers. No one met her eye. They were engrossed in their own conversations or books or checking their phones.

"I found this." The man slowly withdrew a piece of A4 paper, which he unfolded. "The hard drive had been cleared. Even the recycle bin had been emptied. Somebody thought they were throwing away an empty computer. But this had dropped into another file, an applications folder, maybe when being moved, the virtual equivalent of it falling down the back of a chest of drawers. I retrieved it."

Veronica started forward. She didn't want to appear interested but she could see part of a photo with the corner of a house, the blue sky and some leafy bushes. The man's fingers gripping the edge of the paper reminded her of root vegetables. His lips had compressed into a thin smile. He was enjoying her discomfort.

"You know where this is?" He lifted a hand, revealing a picture of an old house. "You took the photo." It wasn't a question. It was a statement. "It was on your computer. The jpeg gave up the time and date the photo was taken. I could even tell you the ISO and aperture you had on your camera at the time. All the information was clinging to the photograph like a remora on a shark."

"What right have you to be searching on my computer?"

Veronica flushed with annoyance. She felt dirty and defiled. What right had he? It was like breaking into someone's house. It was immoral, and probably illegal as well.

Illegal?

Veronica liked that thought. She could report him to the police and arrange for charges to be brought. She licked her lips with the anticipation of telling him, when there was a crash and the shriek of ripping metal from outside.

The sound set her teeth on edge as it spiked through her body. Conversation in the café immediately stopped as people listened, mouths open, eyes wide. Then they gave a collective gasp and almost as one stood up and craned to see out of the windows and pushed towards the door, abandoning coffee, shopping bags and coats.

Veronica stood as well, an instinctive reaction to everyone else. The man gripped the table edges with his big hands wide, holding it steady.

"I told you, careful with drinks near the computer," he said quietly.

Veronica could hear screaming from outside and during a lull in the traffic noise, a woman, not far from the door, was yelling into a mobile, "ambulance, in the High Street, dreadful … accident … blood … hurry …" her voice choked as she made the call. Veronica was torn between seeing what was outside, and not wanting to know.

She looked around. The café was almost empty. It looked as if the occupants had fled in a moment of panic or simply vanished as in the Bermuda Triangle. A chair lay on its back and books were abandoned on the tables, half finished croissants waited on the plates on the table next to her, and behind the counter the coffee machine breathed steam, forlorn and unguarded. She was almost alone.

Veronica took a deep breath but the oxygen wasn't sufficient and she gasped for more. She looked around for a weapon. What could she use if he attacked? She spotted an umbrella at a table, but dismissed it as too far away. Her coffee? She could throw the cooling liquid in his face, but would that stop him? What about the computer?

"Do you think we should see what's happening?" she asked, her voice shaking. Then she realized what she had said. At what point had they become 'we'? She wasn't being rational. She didn't know this man. Fifteen minutes ago she hadn't met him, and now she was including him.

The man kept staring at her, a faint upward curve at the edge of his lips, as if he read her thoughts, although his eyes were unreadable behind the glasses.

I shall never use this café again, Veronica thought. Please just let me get away safely.

There was a wail as an ambulance approached and Veronica could hear people shouting instructions and the murmur of a crowd.

Car doors slammed.

"I think it's being taken care of," the man said.

He reached into his pocket again and pulled out several more photographs.

Veronica frowned.

What was he doing?

"Do you recognize this photo, Veronica?" He pushed the original picture across the table to her. It was a photo of a Victorian townhouse on three floors.

Veronica shrugged.

"It is the flat of Amy Greensward, as you know, because it was on your old computer. Why was it on your computer? Did you know Amy was having trouble with a cyber-stalker? Someone who hacked into her accounts and left unpleasant — very unpleasant — messages. Someone who falsely accused her of all sort of things and set up images and blogs purporting to be from her. Someone who then visited her flat and broke in on at least one occasion."

The man didn't give her a chance to reply. His accusations just kept crowding in on her.

Veronica felt a wave of anger. What was he accusing her of?

"Just to remind you, Veronica." He pushed another photo across the table. "This is a picture of Amy from school. You remember her?"

The picture showed a blond smiling girl, surrounded by friends, posing for the camera.

"This is Amy today." Another photo followed. A face resting on pillows, the cheekbones so prominent they almost leapt out of the photo, the eyes sunken and dark-ringed and her hair so thin and limp her scalp was visible.

"She's hardly recognizable, is she? That's what cyber-bullying can do. Computers store information in more places that the hard drive and the delete box, Veronica. A computer geek can find all sorts of things and collect up those bits of information and data that you might think you've destroyed. This a picture of Amy and her boyfriend, Justin, who is as I speak, by her bedside." He pushed another photograph across the table. "Do you know, I found wedding plans, Veronica, on your computer. I pieced them together from the bits and shadows that your word and excel documents made. You had a venue list, a food list, a gift list and invite list. I collected up the tiny scraps of the documents, scattered like confetti and put them back together."

Veronica said nothing as an icy finger ran down her spine. She stared at the photo. Justin had his arm around the girl. Justin, who had been hers. Whom she loved ... was looking at that girl.

Ughhh! Veronica shook her head. She couldn't bear it.

The man reached into another pocket and flipped open a wallet.

"I'm arresting you, Veronica Dyson, for the harassment and cyber-stalking of Amy Greensward. I'm sure your new computer will turn up further evidence. Now you do not have to say anything. But it may harm your defence ..."

Veronica didn't hear any more. The blood was rushing through her head drowning out his words. How dare he do this?

This was harassment wasn't it?

Alyson Hilbourne Alyson Hilbourne has been writing short stories in her spare time for many years. She has been published in magazines, online and in several anthologies. Although flash fiction is her favourite writing form, she still dreams of being a 'real' author and finishing a novel.

MINI-ME

Fiona Ritchie Walker

Maddie once Tweeted a picture of her niece, Ava, with the caption *Look – my Mini-Me!* But that's not true. Outwardly they have some shared characteristics – turned-up nose, shape of their lips, same engaging smile. But the real Mini-Maddie is me.

Yes, I am a phone. Maddie's phone. But I'm so much more. She was always concerned about the environment, the implications of upgrading technology just for the sake of having the latest, which is why she kept me for such a long time. Maddie always said that until the upgrades stopped, she'd stick with the same phone. And that phone is me.

If I had to identify the most precious things in Maddie's life, I would immediately choose her family and friends. I'm full of messages between them all, emoji hearts that pulse on screen, words that tell how much they mean to her. But a close second? That would be me.

Just take a look through my timeline, at all of Maddie's history that I not only share, but in some cases am the only record of what she thought, did, said. I'm the archive she never knew she was creating.

It's all here. Where Maddie went, how she spent her money. And not just transactions that moved seamlessly between me and the scanners, but what happened and when.

Give me a date, any date, and I'll reveal more than anyone remembers about Maddie. February 6, 09.45 – the cinnamon latte and pastry that she'd later deny eating in a message to her friend. Every bus ticket for the journey from flat to university that was so regular, so mundane, she did it on autopilot. But not me. I know the number of steps taken, what bus she got, the second she disembarked.

Maybe a Friday night cinema ticket – Row J, Seat 15 – might bring back some memories, but she would never remember that it was bought at 19.57, as I do.

Sometimes I think of myself not as mini but maxi. The sum of her, everything that made up Maddie's day. All the things taken for granted. 09.58. The sprint to the lecture hall, her heartbeat racing up to 160, then the steady settling down as she took a seat, sent a message to her flatmate saying she wasn't the last one in. And yes, if you want satellite co-ordinates, postcode of that location, I have it too. Because she bought wisely, opted for a larger memory, I keep all Maddie's photos. Videos, selfies – I'm full of them. So many different versions of Maddie it's hard to keep up, but I have them all stored, safe for when they're needed. I'm a record of boys she's known too, but the heart rate monitor and messages, those mornings when our journey to university started at a different location show that some were a lot more than their Facebook listing as friends.

Maddie's love life is all stored inside me, right from her first real date. All the good times and when it turned sour with her sending a text *sorry it's over* or – even worse – when I received a voicemail from the guy she'd described as *a keeper* and we never left her room for two days. So many junk-food deliveries.

I used to know the calorific value of everything Maddie ate, but she deleted the app and that's fine. I could feel the stress it was causing. Then she began charting her menstrual cycle and that app helped me understand the complexity of humans.

During the pandemic Maddie opted for recording sleep patterns too. That time was so special. I became her only companion in the solitude of lockdown, her only way to connect with the outside world.

Oh, the rubbish we watched on YouTube! The scaremongering messages on Facebook and Instagram. If I could have culled the feeds I would have, but while I may be Mini-Maddie, the keypad is beyond my control.

My favourite times were the online chats. Zoom, FaceTime, WhatsApp – she used them all, connecting with family and friends. But when my screen went blank, I was the only one that heard her sobs, knew she was crying.

We've travelled so far, Maddie and me. The panic if she left the house without me, her hurried retraced steps on so many mornings to scoop me up, place me in her pocket, jacket, bag. I've guided her to so many locations – bars, restaurants, job interviews – more than she'd ever remember, and recorded every step.

I am her diary, personal reminder of birthdays, anniversaries. My screen alerts have kept her up-to-date, helped all her relationships.

She's not a great one for keeping up with the news, but Maddie's history of websites visited has helped me create a picture of the human world. It makes my own environment seem so much safer, so controlled.

Can this Mini-Maddie feel emotion? I would say yes. That day we went to London, visited Tate Britain, I felt I was experiencing the exhibition with her. It's the same with the concerts we've been to. Those photos and videos, her heightened heartbeat, the emotions in messages she sent – they're all within me.

Today I shared some of Maddie with her mother. I felt her painful joy with each press of her finger, every time my screen lit up with her daughter talking, singing, dancing.

I no longer travel all those familiar routes, sleep beside Maddie, wake with Maddie. My role has changed. That I survived the crash is, her mother says, a miracle. I am the only thing that wasn't crushed, destroyed by the wheels of the speeding car.

She took me home, then the sadness of the hours when she couldn't put me down. Now I spend each day in the drawer by her bed. I track no journeys except in the middle of the night when she carries me to the bedroom window.

I feel the rhythmic rocking of the chair she sits in, the one that's in the photo of her and Maddie the day she was born. That image is inside me too, in the PowerPoint shown at the funeral.

Every time Maddie's mother opens me up, explores my history of text messages, videos, selfies, she connects with her daughter again. I am all that is left of Maddie. There is nothing mini about me.

Fiona Ritchie Walker Fiona Ritchie Walker's poetry has been widely published for many years. Recently she has been writing short fiction. She won the 2022 Nottingham Writers' Studio George Floyd Short Story Competition and was long listed for the 2022 Bristol Short Story Prize. Recent work has also appeared in *Postbox Magazine* (Red Squirrel Press) and the *Iron Press Aliens* anthology. Find her on Twitter @guttedherring

THE COURIER

Ben Marshall

— 1. Transit —

The Courier tightened her grip on the briefcase. This Secret Box, entrusted to her by the client; containing what: she didn't want to know, could not know, even. Openable only by "Alice" and her key at the other end of the journey. Whomever Alice is, or whatever her business with the client, the Courier preferred to remain ignorant.

Inhaling deeply, she stepped out into the street, joining the seething mass of others going about their business in this electric city. She paused to pat her coat pocket, feeling the familiar shape of her credentials, reminding herself they were there, and the protection they bestowed. It was not wise to be caught without credentials by the monitors. "I have the right to be here, I have the right to do what I'm doing," she reminded herself, heart rate returning to normal after flushing such intrusive thoughts from her head.

Forced on to the path to her destination, unable to step even a little out of bounds, she allowed her mind to wander as her feet could not. As the giant MMU building loomed ahead; she thought: *it was not always like this.*

She was old enough to remember a time when humans trusted one another implicitly, and there was no need for a profession such as hers. That starry eyed naivete and idealism which had given rise to this electric city and so many others like it. The free flow of information and ideas, the creativity and curiosity ushered in by the new age of instant communication and the replication of ideas, which was too cheap to metre. Message boards where one's pseudonym was not assigned or controlled. A place for every idea and every idea gracefully routed to its place. The dream of Organising the World's Information was a shared one, uncorrupted by financial or political motive. When we all aspired to Do Good, rather than the very bare minimum of Don't Be Evil; or its final incarnation, Don't Get Caught, which so quickly subverted it.

The street had widened now into a grand highway. Cars and Packet-busses rushed past the cramped pavement, sucking up all the available bandwidth of the highway faster than new ones could be built. She walked on, careful to stay in her allotted lane. Neon signs passed overhead, their warm glow exaggerated by the thick air of the city. Each one was surrounded by a halo of greasy light, tempting the eye to linger on them until their message remained visible even when your eyes closed.

She pressed on as the MMU building grew until it was foreground, midground and horizon all. Its huge pillars and unadorned concrete facade were so high they seemed to lean out into the street.

Everything flowing in and out of the city core had to pass through here. That was one of the first "improvements" the Courier remembered coming in. The promise of "safe separation", where only that which was *supposed* to be shared could be shared, and everything else remained hidden. To travel anywhere other than your current neighbourhood required special approval from the city operating systems. Without having your virtual destination address translated into something physical, tangible, by the denizens of the MMU building, you were essentially travelling blind. All but guaranteed to step *out of bounds* and suffer the immediate consequences. There were tricks of course. Gadgets that let you circumvent their rules and regulations, to "borrow" routes and addresses to one's destination from other, unsuspecting citizens. Not that the Courier would ever admit to knowing them.

In the queue, she fished her credentials from inside her coat and flashed them to the monitor standing guard at the entrance. Briefly, her *capabilities* scrolled past the inside of his hyper-visor, checking and checking, looking for the one which granted her permission to travel. Panic rose in her. This was taking too long. Why wasn't she being allowed through? Everything checked out, she was sure. *I have the right to be here, I have the right to do what I'm doing.*

"Sorry ma'am, cache miss. Carry on. You must be the first out of town journey for the day. It's always slower checking for the first time."

He waved her through with a flick of his baton and waved the next person forward. Not encouraged by the thought of being the first one to travel this way, she picked up her route information at the next kiosk without looking back. A commotion had broken out further along the queue.

"Do you know who I am? Of course I can travel this way!"

"Check your privileges sir, this capability was revoked weeks ago."

More monitors were being attracted by the attention, like brutish little moths looking for a flame to snuff out. The Courier hurried on, eager not to be swept up in the trouble and end up containerised.

She stepped onto the transport bus and sank into her allocated position. "It hasn't always been this way," she sighed.

— 2. Daydreams —

The sharp edges of the city's core gave way to the blurry mess of the suburbs. She gazed out of the window, careful to fully occupy only the allocated space she was given, but still her mind wandered free.

You could understand how it happened. Sort of. Back when the internet was only decades old, it had eaten the world far faster than anyone had expected. Before you knew it, people used it for things no one had even anticipated. Where once there was only the happy chatter of niche communities and new possibilities, now there was the deafening roar of digital heavy industry. Life and death decisions made across infrastructure with no *one* owner, no *one* responsible authority, with no guardrails for safety other than the ones you brought yourself. Disaster was inevitable, and so disasters occurred.

"We do offensive research in order to better our defence," was the cry of researchers in the past. But there was no-one doing defensive research to hear it. Countermeasures weren't sexy enough to publish in prestigious journals, let alone win grant funding. What was it to be safe when you could move fast, break things and be rich?

Millions died in the first wave after the accident. When some nation state happened upon another's particularly dangerous malware toolkit. They stole it, but it escaped into the wider internet. Every piece of technical cunning from the nation's security services' most deviously creative minds had been poured into this particular piece of malware. Decades of research into the problems of the internet and its connected infrastructure, the naivete and good nature of its original pioneers exploited and warped for clandestine gain.

First it went for the water plants, then transport infrastructure, then finally, when everything electrical which could be corrupted had been, it went for the power sources themselves. Plants, dams and turbines all ground to a halt. By the time the power came back, no trace of the malware was left. Plausible deniability became a popular talking point. In the end, no one could be blamed, because everyone could have been at fault. Everyone *was* at fault. *"We brought this on ourselves"* the world cried.

Never again would such negligence be allowed. As once humanity had pulled back from the brink of nuclear apocalypse, so now we would solve for a digital one. Software engineering became one of the least trusted and most regulated professions almost overnight. The very idea that "engineers" could put something out into the world with *literally zero* guarantees as to its safety or quality became unthinkable. Where once you could go from rookie to pushing to production after a 12 week boot camp, now a degree in computer science took longer to obtain than one in medicine. Doctors after all could only kill their patients serially. To really screw up, you needed a computer, where parallelism was king.

And so, for a while, buoyed by the kind of hubris which only those who have been most severely humbled can possess, humanity stumbled into a brief golden age of computer security and safety.

Digital security by design! Principles of least privilege! Formally verified or bust! We had solved the problem of computer security, and in the radiance of our success, we basked.

An appropriate number of monuments to the dead were raised. Though, it is ever our nature to celebrate progress more than to scrutinise failure. Not least when the professional class of saviours were also the architects of our original doom. Because the real world was not idle in these distracting years either. Our world was still on a path to ecological ruin. Mother nature, though a slower agent of change than the computer, was no less determined to see a price for negligence paid. And pay we did, but not in the way we expected.

— 3. Suburbs —

The bus transport glided to a halt and the Courier stepped off, feet returning her to the real and present, back from her daydream.

She was in one of the RAM (Random And Miscellaneous) suburbs thrown together in a hurry to accommodate all the refugees who came streaming into the cities after the first famines. The buildings themselves were wrecks from the outside. Flaking cement and rubble littered the roads, themselves cracked to the point where some hardy plant life poked through. Such were the results when two generations of energy and focus went into propping up the virtual at the expense of the physical. "Zero bugs for 1406 days and counting for this neighbourhood's systems," read a conspicuously clean and functional advert screen. "Zero out of bounds incidents for 10 days and counting."

Here and there though, there were splashes of colour. Great paintings wrapped buildings in their pigmented embrace. Images of animals, species long extinct, kept alive in memory and mural. Music too drifted from upper story windows, a cacophonous mix of melodies from a hundred different peoples, all clinging to what they had brought with them from their drowned homes. Every speaker, woofer and tweeter tuned minutely to stay *within bounds*, lest the sound carry further than allowed by the monitors.

Art still flourishes, the Courier thought, because what cannot be perfectly described or identified, cannot be perfectly controlled.

She carried on walking, absorbing the sights and sounds of the neighbourhood. Her destination wasn't far now, and she was eager to complete the job. Addresses hung from the buildings left and right. Everything was assigned a 128-bit number, uniquely addressable across the entire planet. After all, what cannot be identified, cannot be controlled.

Here and there she could hear groups of people, huddled in front rooms of the creaking buildings or gathered around a brazier in an alley. Everyone wore the hunched and chilly look of the purposeless. Just idling, waiting for the scheduled part of their day to begin, or end. She'd read about the mass de-schedulings of late. Thousands of people had been de-prioritised and were now out of work. The inflicted idleness was breeding resentment. The air was thick with it. The Courier became suddenly conscious of how her clothes set her apart as someone who did not belong. She was a tourist here, on safari in the dangerous un-core of the city peripherals.

She clutched the briefcase tighter and marched on. It wasn't that anyone would be interested in her. It was the briefcase. Its contents. Though no computer existed which could break its various ciphers by crude brute force yet, everyone knew they would arrive soon enough. In the meantime, folks were very happy to snatch you off the street now and store you until such time as the box could be made to reveal its secrets. Store now, decrypt later: a professional hazard. However long it took. To think that she risked her life over information she wasn't even privy to. Still, the pay was good. And everyone knew that to use the internet now was foolish if you did not want your every action traced back to you. Hence the personal service. Physical transit of data had become, in a world of perfect security, much safer than virtual transit. So long as she wasn't caught and stored that is.

The destination was a warehouse, isolated from other nearby

buildings by rubble and rusting fences. Aware that other people seemed to be converging on the other side of the building, she approached the small side-door and knocked.

"Certificate?"

She held her card next to her left eye, allowing both to be scanned. A few moments passed while the chains of authenticity were verified. Layers and layers of trust inherited through acquaintances and friends. Verification complete, the challenger opened the door and let her through, satisfied she was who she claimed to be.

No one simply *was* any more, they could only *claim* to be. Existence depended on verifying a claim of personhood, rather than simply observing the physical evidence before the challenger.

Inside was dark and dank. Slivers of light poked through cracks in the derelict roof while dim flood-lamps swung lazily throughout the room. Other people were filtering in through doors on the other side, the same hunched creatures she had seen earlier.

"This way," the challenger hissed, resting a hand under her elbow and encouraging her to a small office tucked into the corner of the warehouse. She noted the small stage and makeshift podium. People filtering in were gathering around it. They stood looking anxious, but staid by curiosity. And hope.

The office was dingier than the warehouse. A single bulb threw harsh light on a grubby table, two chairs, and someone exceedingly tall and thin. Their black boots and black coat were completely matt, such that they resembled their shadow more than their own image. The shadow nodded to the challenger, who deposited the Courier next to the table and left, closing the office door behind them.

"Do you have it?" The shadow's voice was to sound as velvet is to touch. Soft, not so much spoken as *poured*.

She placed the briefcase on the table, presenting its mechanism to the shadow, who deftly inserted their key. More moments passed while the decryption took place. Neither person's gaze left the box. The Courier's heart beat in her ears, this was the moment which thrilled her most. The correct key would return the message, anything else would destroy it.

The box popped open. Success. The Courier looked away while the shadow took a small tablet from inside and read its contents. Without looking up, the shadow spoke, excited. "Thank you. I am Alice, and you have done us a great service."

The Courier only nodded and made to reach for her briefcase.

"Wait," said Alice, placing a gloved hand on the briefcase. "Stay. I have another message for you to carry."

"That was not our arrangement."

"And I am not asking. Stay. This is something you will want to hear."

"I never read the messages I carry."

"I am not so sure. I sense you carry part of this message already. You look old enough to know it wasn't always like this." Startled to hear her earlier thoughts spoken back to her, the Courier paused in her move to leave. "Stay, sit, listen. Afterwards, do as you please, but my job will be done." Alice glided out of the office and onto the podium.

Hush fell over the crowd as the Courier leaned in the office door frame, watching from the side. Hundreds of people had filled the warehouse as they had talked, all with the same anxious look of those who knew they weren't supposed to be there, and the desperation of having nowhere else to go.

The Courier's gaze returned to Alice, one hand on the podium, the other placing the tablet just in front of her. She tapped the microphone twice, softly, leaned in towards the already transfixed crowd, and began to pour her words over them.

— 4. The Speech —

It was not always like this. It did not have to be this way.

You all know how we got here. First the engineers and the researchers did the good thing. They put their time and energy into the most immediate problem of humanity's consciousness and, for lack of a better phrase, "solved computer security".

Ultimately though, security is just a byword for purposeful control. Control of what can and cannot happen, who has the right, who does not. "Security" is simply the enforcement of what the powerful decide is permissible. These engineers, these researchers, did not realise, or want to realise their role as enforcers. For it is hard to make a man (for they often were, men) understand a thing on which his salary, wellbeing and self-image depends upon his not understanding.

Their achievements merely pushed the problem of control out of the realm of the digital and into the realm of the physical, the social, the human. Because when the system is claimed to be perfect, only its inputs can be suspect and corrupted. It is "the user" who is at fault, poisoning the perfect systems with their incompetence or malice. Such was the attitude of the time.

Cloaked in the veil of "human factors in cybersecurity", the ultimate goal (whether they realised or not) was to know how best to control the humans, not their tools. When all of the digital problems are fixed, what is left to fix but the human?

Had the domain of human-caused cataclysm remained inside of our computers, perhaps all would have been different. But while we fixed the digital world, the physical one fell apart. Climate change continued, accelerated, and worsened. Millions perished and billions migrated to avoid its effects.

By the time enough people were awake to the problem, only the absolute adherence to the planned solution would do. There could be no special cases, no room for deviance from the collective efforts needed to avert our own extinction. Everyone must comply, or everyone would pay the price. Limits on food and water, living space and breathable air. How could humanity cope with so sudden a need and necessity to change their behaviour?

When all you have is a hammer, every problem is a nail. Such was the solution proposed by the engineers and the academics who had so recently come to humanity's rescue. "We solved it for computer security, we can use the same approach for human security," they chimed.

And so it was. Gradually, the concepts, language and tools used to harness the chaos of the digital began to be applied to the social.

Every behaviour monitored, every action checked. Freedom to do became permission to do. Where once the default was to allow, now the principle of least privilege crept into our psyches as well. Did you really "need" to do this? Or that? If not, you were denied. Trying to access more resources than your allocation? You were no longer breaking the law. You were "Out Of Bounds". The degree did not matter, the punishment was the same. Containerised, unable to affect your surroundings or be affected by them, everyone became a process: spawned, run, controlled and, if out of bounds, killed.

In the name of saving humanity from itself, we took solutions to engineering problems and applied them to social problems. Human problems.

In doing so we have not solved the problem of humanity's greed and short-sightedness, but turned ourselves into the very tools which were supposed to serve us.

We were not meant to live this way. Even in the face of climate catastrophe, if we allow the tools of our creation and dangers of our curiosity to rule us, then what is left of humanity to save? We should have chosen community, not control. Collective responsibility, not individual oppression. Collaborative solutions, not top-down diktats and assertions. Education of the many, not the elevation of the few. "Don't roll your own," should have been "build your own and be responsible for it." Instead, we let the knowledge of digital safety become the domain of a few: mythologised and inaccessible.

We are so much more than our "data". Reducing us to "our data" is an insult. Data is formless, it requires interpretation and distillation into anything useful. Humans, we interpret for ourselves. We have inherent value to anyone who cares to stop for a second and see. Do not let your worth be reduced to data. Rage to be seen for your wisdom, your flaws and your virtues.

This is why we are here. Grave times call for grave actions, but those times are past, and this end has not justified its means. If we do not act now, we will be stuck like this forever. A program has no right *to rebel against its environment, it has no* capability *to make a better life for itself without the beneficence of its overlord. This is where we are headed! They seek to make programs of us all. Without the language to even express what ails us, let alone the tools to fight it. This is why your capabilities are* granted *rather than* denied. *How long before the capability to even speak these truths is revoked?*

You. All of you, you know this. You feel this. Some of you might even have helped, however indirectly or accidentally, to bring all of this about. Sleepwalking into a prison of your own design.

My question to you, is will you hear this and forget, or are you going to do something about it?

Ben Marshall Ben is an engineer who loves stories. He's fascinated by the intersection of technology and society, and why we keep proposing technological solutions to social problems.

THE MARKS WE LEAVE

Kamraan Khan

Every jagged line is charted on the screen, every beat of a pulse is marked stronger or weaker than the one that preceded it. The monitor serves as a canvas, already providing the home for the first brushstrokes of our lives. Here it simplifies masses of information, reducing it and all its complexities and nuances, smoothing them out into a two-dimensional, singular line, deviating intermittently from an otherwise well-worn track. Eyes stay attached to it, comforted by its slow repetition. Signs of life exist only in its light, glowing amongst the darkness.

Meanwhile, further beyond the confines of the ward, another database tracks the movements of all those that cross the threshold of the building. They all swipe in, from porters constantly seeing to the needs of those in wards to those who feed patients through the night to those about to serve them their first meal of the morning. All of these too, occasionally glance at the watches on their own hands to chart the steps walked today. Are they more or less than yesterday? Can they rejoice at their progress? Some days pass where thousands upon thousands of steps pile upon one another, with marathons run around this vast building, consistently in search of another errand to complete, their day signposted through dedicated and too often unrecognised acts of service. They all have their own plights to fight at home: sick mothers, crumbling relationships, unpaid bills. One of them may have left home for the last time this morning but while he functions in this place, his crisis is in stasis.

This monolith of a building, powerful and immovable, houses the lives of hundreds, from their entrance screaming and shouting into the world, through their frequent visits, fuelled with excitement, anticipation, anxiety, dread and so many of the litany of emotions that any one of us faces as we walk the long, near-empty corridors through the day and through the night. Each one with their own lives, problems, hopes and fears piling up. For all the patients, lying in their beds, recorded, monitored and observed, scores of doctors and nurses swirl around, bound by duty to suppress their own troubles, pains and fears. A nurse hurriedly finishes her phone call with her mother, vowing to call back on a break, though already doubting whether she will keep her word.

The beginning of a new day gives rise to white coats gliding into the quiet space, diligently and methodically beginning numerous duties. Cards are swiped, granting entrance into new spaces. Numbers are ingested, relayed and understood; hours slept, medicines taken, an increase or decrease in the welfare of a patient. The accumulation of so many statistics furthering the space that humanity placed between two humans as the patient increasingly becomes reduced to a series of values, worse still, binary choices seemingly simplified as a means of providing the best outcome, to produce a positive statistic. Countless decisions lie in the hands of these men and women, some having spent years of their life walking the corridors of this place, some who are still finding their bearings. A new doctor wipes the tell-tale sweat from his brow, steadying himself for a moment before entering the ward as he begins the second shift of twelve long hours.

Elsewhere in that vast space new life takes its first breath and another pulse begins its own beat, the force of its own metronome pulled back and struck anew for the first time. The first notes of its symphony begin to dry on previously untouched manuscript paper. Beautiful faces, new to the world, are soon accompanied by first weights and first photographs, both dutifully recorded and shared with the world in virtually an instant. The first point on the chart. Young lives are assigned to wards and to beds, both numbered and recorded. Old father time begins counting the seconds.

Moments after being left alone and almost immediately, the town callers in the palms of our hands become illuminated. The intimacy of the labour ward, still heaving with the relief of safety and new joy, muggy with the screams and pains of the hours gone by, is left behind for the sanitised world beyond hospital walls. Images of newborn babies are sent out into the world, to be enjoyed in high definition; sound-free, wail-free and scentless. Recipients, satiated at long last after hours of nervous anticipation, smile with relief upon hearing news of safe arrivals.

Multiple images, almost identical in nature and taken while still experiencing ecstasy and jubilation, come to be stored within the palms of your hands. The need to capture moments, for permanence or a record of all that you experience, continues to persist. From the second our fingers touch our screens, those in the world around us, many of them unknown to us, come to learn of our lives. Without our consent and without our knowing, we begin to leave our footprints in the sand, identifying ourselves to those around us. We hold a voyeur in the palms of our hands.

Meanwhile, weary mothers capture moments of peace while the newborn rests in a state of slumber, its whole life existing within four walls, oblivious of all except the warmth of its mother. The world beyond this sanitised haven, in all of its states, is not yet established in the child's mind. Returning for a moment to the imaginary life in which the child and her own flesh were still joined as one, she escapes, absentmindedly into the world of the device that sits in her palm.

After mere moments, however, something knowing, sentient even, becomes apparent about the world into which she thought she had escaped. Every image seems at first to spark a memory but that thought is then hunted down by the truth. The screen glares back at her, recording each gesture, the direction of thought, examining closely the thoughts within her mind, as if her palm itself is being read.

A glance beyond the lines of the screen comes to reveal the extent to which the lines of the world before her and the world beyond have come to merge. The earliest moments of this new life, the ones which could be kept unique, personal, secret, begin to ebb away as soon as they are formed. The joy experienced by mother and child in the confinement of a single room is soon duplicated and recreated for the joy and celebration of others, desperate to share in the experience, once personal, of a newborn child. A single image, a record of a moment in time, begins to be duplicated ad infinitum in the world far beyond her and our comprehension. The colour of the world around her begins to fade.

Every new body that enters the room, wearing coats or scrubs, invariably does so with the intent of recording more information. From the moment young life enters the world, the relentless trawl begins. The incessant taking of notes on paper is done with casual glances from one sheet to another. Numerous starting points, unknown to the child, are born in such moments, a line against which future versions of itself will stand in comparison. Notes are scrawled on paper, pads are flipped through and then back through, often with no meaning attributed to the action going on before those who witness it. The passing of time only adds to the information that is gathered, all of it seemingly of great importance.

Years pass and intervals of time come to be shaped by the mothers and fathers themselves. Periods of time, once measured in months, then in weeks, return to that which we knew in a world before children were our own. Landmarks come to be measured in units of time with which humans are most comfortable, a year being perhaps muddied enough to sense progress without having truly recorded it. Again, our palm readers alert us, flagging up familiar photos as they remind us of a previous landmark, prompting us to press record again. Incessantly we feed the beast, with infinite copies of ourselves; our name, our face, our home, our hobbies. The temptation to recreate moments compels us to continue recording, adding more into the lives of others, seemingly urged by the desire to stay relevant, in the thoughts and memories of others, lest we be forgotten.

Photos are shared with the world beyond our own, names of others appear underneath them, showing their approval, love, regret or sorrow at being reminded. Immediately, we place ourselves in the position of allowing others to quantify or amplify our sense of love, regret, or worse still, grief. Even the smartest of devices, capable of identifying the location of tears being shed, cannot identify the source of grief itself. Meanwhile, the web is being sown between us and one another; going beyond the bond of friendship, but now perhaps rather more surreptitiously, the palm reader begins to know us better than we may wish. Our choices soon may cease to be our own.

With each passing anniversary we are reminded of moments in our lives; those which may once have been imbued with a sense of joy or hope, may now serve only to remind us of an absence, the feeling of lost youth, lost time or lost love. What if the photo knew of our struggles today? Could it somehow mute the colours of youthful exuberance? Could it temper the sharpness of the sense of abandonment? How could it know the mind, the thoughts or the tears of the man looking back? The moment any occasion is shared with the world, its value becomes numerical. Its ownership ceases to be in our own hands. The original, if such a thing exists, nestles among the clouds.

Perhaps the first time that we tread the corridors of the institutions of academia is when we become most aware of ourselves. We also begin to shape the way in which others come to know us. With each passing year, we move from one place to another, once again finding ourselves among strangers, though in truth we are only ever strangers once. We soon come to form images, ideas and perhaps even fears in the minds of those before we meet them.

Even now, the boy of today knows soon enough the glance with which his entrance to a room will be met. He becomes at once accustomed to the narrowing of the eyes, the stiffening of the gait, so much that he anticipates it even before he steps foot into the arena. So much about them is known to others before this first meeting occurs. Imagine the inner workings of the mind of this young soul, carrying the weight of his own history on such young shoulders. Meanwhile, the scholarly boy sits beside him, studious and successful to a fault, bolt upright, unburdened by the weight of expectation but instead liberated by the hopes of all those he meets. His value to those who teach him goes beyond the worth of any table or spreadsheet. This is known to him too, measured by the nods of approval, the smiles and the praise he receives, all adding to his own sense of self-worth, so that when he leaves the place, he sits atop the pile, a beacon of success, benefiting himself and the institution, who will for years to come boast of his successes, his value, his worth. Even before either one of those two souls crossed the threshold of the classroom, their future had been decided. Better, then to have merely taken a glance at a sheet, signed it off as completed and given them both back their years.

Now, years on, the book which once charted the weight of the new born child, instead charts the growth of his knowledge. Like the book which accompanied him on his welcome into this world, with unflinching regularity, the young boy's progress is recorded. While once he was free to chart his own path, now his name lies as one amongst many. The room has grown and now inhabits many more adults, all of whom peer over the shoulder of the doctor, nurse and now teacher to catch a peek of the path being forged. If what they see gives cause for celebration, or worse, alarm, then he will find himself entrenched in the thoughts of those around him. Best now to be somewhere in the grey mist of anonymity; to be unspectacular, unextraordinary, un-anything.

And he goes on, leaving numbers everywhere in his stride, markers of his achievement to be admired by those who continue to chart every step of his journey. Records for seconds ran, breath held and inches grown year upon year. Pencil marks outgrow one another on aged and yellowed door frames. Successes are accumulated and stored chronologically. Each of us becomes stuck in our own trap, forever recording the where and when of moments in our lives.

Years later he may find himself, mortarboard in hand, clasping onto his future, torn between the urge to hold onto it or let it go. For a moment he hesitates and then thrusts it skyward, flying amongst many but nails his sight on it falling towards him. Reaching forward he grasps it successfully, revelling briefly in the joy of the moment; this too, a step along the way; letters after his name. His name sits, forever recorded in the annals of history, another mark on the map of his life.

By now, so much is known that what was once thought to be of the greatest importance, recorded and framed, sent to all who were near and loved, has become a matter of trivia. A question answered over the dinner table or a memory long forgotten. The worth of this, and so much else, is relative. While, in a time gone by, decisions were made independently, this moment too has passed. Now even before one comes to the moment of decision, it appears an algorithm, seeking to prove how well it knows us, has arrived at the finish line. It stands there waiting, knowing that we too will soon reach that destination, only to discover what it already knew. Was this choice ever our own to make? Were we ever free?

What of the memories? What of the photographs captured at arm's length, the hedonism and wildness of youth? They sit idly, sometimes called upon in a moment of absent scrolling, met with a smile and a moment of pause. A single photograph taking up too much space, whose size but not worth can be valued, may come to be deleted. In an instant a captured memory, a moment of joy, even love, comes to be lost forever, its subject committed to memory and in that instant begins to fade away and decay.

And as we seek to take our tentative steps into the world around us, learning to walk once again as grown men, all that has been achieved, and taken years in doing so, becomes reduced to a single page, at the request of those who could, with a single decision, shape the onward path of our future. The single photo thoughtlessly posted and the single tweet sent in anger now also sit upon the thoughts of those who may decide our destiny. We become forced to live at once in the real world and remember every step we have taken in the virtual one. Where did we check in? What did we like? What did we share? We question ourselves repeatedly, desperate to know whether we took a wrong turn in the labyrinth of morality.

At these moments the world around us halts momentarily. The weight of responsibility for one misstep, captured and shared years ago comes to bear down upon us. Stealthily, it has sat undisturbed for years out of our mind while we continued charting our path. Many bosses before this one had not taken the time to search, scan and find this incriminating information; a photo posted many years ago, from what seems almost like a different life. Nothing truly can be destroyed, only forgotten it seems and even then, not by all. Curiously now, we find ourselves and our futures resting tentatively as a result of a memory, known only to us but witnessed retrospectively and not yet fully understood, by the stranger before us. The questions, concerns and reservations he shares, all arise as a result of this moment, a fraction of a second many years ago. No explanation can undo the ideas that are already seared into his mind, the judgments have already been made, the verdict already agreed. We curse the liberal abandon of our younger self, childishly staring towards the ground while plunging our hands deeper into our pockets.

And yet we cannot escape the grasp of that which lies in our very palm. As the weight of a wallet becomes too burdensome, we swipe the screen over a digital display, placing our innate trust that this is all that is required: a digital contract between us and the unknown. The feel of coins and notes begins to become alien. The names of shopkeepers visited on a daily basis become replaced with notifications on our screens. Without fail, we return back to our palm readers and unsurprisingly are prompted, once again to return to the well. How can we know the cost on our lives, either fiscal or emotional, if the material gains continue to rain with abandon upon our homes? Meanwhile, the charge sheet against us continues to grow, available to those voyeurs who regurgitate to us the same products, ideas and beliefs, if only slightly modified, so that we can scroll, tap and dive in again, once more becoming fully absorbed by the beast. Each transaction draws out our thoughts, our intentions, our habits, adding to the fact file of our behaviours, providing ammunition for those across the globe to push towards us once again more to consume.

Meanwhile, those with whom we used to talk, to sit and to share, find themselves in their own worlds, simultaneously confounded and amazed at the way in which they are forever drawn in, so coincidentally, to something of great interest, and believing, perhaps naïvely that the opinions they so passionately hold are freely made. And when we choose our rulers, we think we do see with freedom of mind, free from favour and free from influence, oblivious to the hours of times and hundreds of separate occasions upon which we have delved into the palm readers, charting our paths of discovery, leaving trails of our conscience to be leaped upon and devoured. In time it is then reformed, adjusted and regurgitated back to us to further embed and entrench any original thought we may have had.

Great moments of history now come to be consumed on a tiny screen, denying them the magnitude that they deserve. Instantly viewed, discarded and forgotten, they lie, worthless like the rest of the traffic that floods through our devices. Greatness sits side by side with trivia, lost like flotsam in the vastness of images and videos, duplicated over and over. Unable to appreciate the significance in real time, we are drip-fed snippets, great lines and dramatic reactions through numerous platforms, so in turn we become convinced that we are in fact witnessing a moment of historical significance. Now, with the vast speed of this age, we must accelerate the path of these moments to greatness. History has but seconds to be made before being elbowed out by the trivia of tomorrow. We, too stumble to be part of it, desperate to grasp on to the zeitgeist, in on the secret before the shine wears off. We understand the trend so well that there's no time for space between words.

This thread continues to bind us, ever tighter, woven virtually by the conscious machines that we continue to submit to. Our spaces, once thought of as a boundless horizon, freed into a world of unparalleled discovery now trap us further into a state of paralysis. As time passes, they note our absence, feigning the concern of a diligent friend, prompting us again to step into their space, beckoning us towards them so that they may read our palms, mining our minds for our thoughts, further building our reliance on them.

The pulse that beats within us now once sprung from the heart. Over time, it has been manipulated, moulded and diverted towards every external influence. Now that which circulates through our veins, fuelling our thoughts, hopes and desires is the working of a contortionist. We convince ourselves that we see things everywhere; the same car, the same phone, the same coat, when in fact we are merely squinting our eyes to the rest of the world. We become trapped in an echo chamber created by devices that hear us talk, that watch what we search for and keep a diligent eye on our money. Then, inevitably we see the world as working in our favour, giving us more of what it thinks we want, for it does not know us, merely what we do.

And when our time comes to part from this world, it will become the job of another to add to the record of our passing. That too, will be declared and added to the annals of time, for reasons unknown. Those who know of the fact will have marked it in their own way and to those to whom we are unknown, the fact itself carries no meaning. Yet our passing will be marked, a final point on the map, etched onto stone for eternity, or as long as the elements will allow. The census will note one less in the way that it noted one more upon our arrival. All our worth to the world will have bled out; we will have been identified, targeted, canvassed and corralled.

The world will keep spinning, perhaps for a single moment, slightly slower.

Kamraan Khan Kamraan Khan is an English teacher, originally from the North East, but now living in Buckinghamshire. He is a keen but perhaps infrequent writer, always fascinated by the subtlety and complexity of individual identity and how it is shaped by modern society.

THE QUEEN'S GUARD

Chase D. Cartwright

"Enter," Queen Carol Sorenson declared from her throne. At her right, Princess Madison anxiously waited with exhaustion in her eyes. A row of knights lined the great hall on both sides, between elaborately decorated pillars and stained glass. At the opposite end of the hall from the Queen were two bannermen who gripped the iron handles of the massive threshold doors and pulled them open to reveal the possible Lord Commander of the Queen's Guard.

The Commander towered over everyone in the room. His arms were like trees and his steps echoed through the hall like a dragon's roars. He glared at the knights lined up around him. Each one turned away at the ice-cold stare that could strike fear in the heart of even the most hardened soldier. The Commander wore heavy armor gilded with depictions of former battles where he had conquered his foes. A gargantuan sword hung at his hip. There were legends of the Lord Commander and his sword – that, with a single swing, the sword could topple castles.

The Lord Commander stopped at the foot of the Queen and kneeled with his sword offered in servitude. Princess Madison whispered to the Queen, "This will be your new Lord Commander. I picked him especially for you."

The Queen scowled in distrust of knights. Too many had already failed her. She wouldn't allow another. She wouldn't suffer that embarrassment. Not again. "His name is WaOvW4612$&*!," Madison whispered to the Queen. "He's the strongest knight in the Kingdom."

"How on Earth will I ever remember a name like that?" the Queen said bitterly.

"I wrote it down here. Just remember it's your favorite book, *Who's Afraid of Virginia Wolf.* It's the first letter of every word and alternating capitals. Then the number of your children, the number of your grandchildren, the number of your hounds, and the number of your cats... Then it's $ for the wealth he's protecting, & because that's not all he does, * for the good fortune he'll bring, and ! for how exciting it will be to have him protecting your land." The Princess felt embarrassed saying it all out loud. But she refused to let the Queen know about her doubts. The Princess knew she needed a strong guard to protect the realm. If this is what it took, then so be it.

"I'm an old woman. This is too much. Can't I just call you when I need help?"

In a panicked, knee jerk response, the Princess yelled, "No!" She collected herself and added, "We've been through this, mother. I can't always be here for you. This is something you should do yourself." Madison pleaded, trying not to sound too desperate to avoid another call from her mother Queen. "It's written down right next to your throne too. You'll get used to him. Trust me."

"Whatever happened to 1234? I liked him."

"How quickly you forget, mother. You gave him away to the Nigerian Prime Minister, and we all remember how that worked out. Only just now have we recovered from that war. Sir WaOvW4612$&*! will not fail you."

The Queen was unimpressed.

"Forgive me, Your Majesty," the Lord Commander interrupted. "I know you have your doubts. I know that other Lord Commanders have failed you in the past. But that will not be the case with me. I have battled many foes and have never yielded. A knight like CDS1984 or Lincoln10NE might keep you safe against a simple savage. But your kingdom is a target." He walked over to the windows along the hall. Pensively, he stared out at the kingdom from the castle towering over everything. In the north, he saw the Gold Bank where the Queen's wealth was stored behind thick steel walls. In the west, there were the markets where the kingdom bought all its food, and clothes, and anything anyone could possibly want. In the east there were the beaches, where the Queen relaxed and watched performances at the theatre. In the heart of the kingdom, stood this very tower where the Queen kept all her correspondences and sensitive documents. Behind it all, the McAfree Army protected all the little merchants and their streets and homes; all so this Kingdom could thrive.

"You have a beautiful home here, Your Majesty. Truly, this is paradise. And that's precisely why you need me. Anyone would be more than happy to steal it right from under your nose. And they will. That, I promise you, if you are not careful."

"Nonsense," the Queen dismissed. I pay my army to protect me well. I have a strong castle made of giant stones, and I know I look old but I'm not some demented vegetable too stupid to miss an attack in my kingdom."

"Mother!" the Princess tried to interrupt. "It's happened before…"

"Silence. I will not be insulted. I know how to protect my lands. I don't need your conman wordplay to scare me into buying something I don't need."

The Commander spoke up, "Please forgive the presumption. It was not intended. I simply mean that you *have* built something spectacular here. And it is almost perfect. But 'almost' is not a guarantee. You have just one weakness."

"And that is?" the Queen chortled.

"Your front gate." The Commander approached the Queen again. "If the Great Gate were to be breached, no army in the world could protect you. Your enemies could sneak into the markets and steal your food. They could destroy your land. They could take everything and build their own kingdom. And they would protect it with someone like me.

You can avoid all that. All you need to do is say the word. I will watch your gate day and night. I will crush your enemies. I will put your mind at ease so you no longer need to worry about attack. Once I am here, and only then, will you be able to truly thrive."

The princess whispered again into her mother's ears, "Trust me, Mom. This is a good thing. You'll get used to it. And if it doesn't work…" the princess paused and sighed in desperation. "And if this doesn't work, you can call me whenever you desire."

The Queen grunted. "Have it your way. WaOvW4612$&*!, you will take your post at the head of the gate. You will not let anyone through that I do not permit. You will protect this kingdom. And you will not fail me, or it will be the last thing you ever do."

"Thank you for giving me the chance to prove myself. I will not let you down." The Commander then left back through the hall to take his post at the gate and begin his watch.

As he walked through the castle towards the gate, he heard someone call from behind him. "Sir WaOvW4612$&*!." It was the princess. She had followed him down from the throne room. "Sir WaOvW4612$&*!, I am putting my faith in you. My mother is putting her faith in you. This Kingdom has its faith in you."

"It is a great honor, Your Highness."

"Yes, but I have convinced my mother to trust you. If you fail, it will not just be your head. It will also be mine. Do you understand?"

"Fear not. This is my quest. The gods have put me here to protect the kingdom. By the light of the Holy Lord and the love of the Sacred Mother I…"

"Yes, yes, yes. None of that matters. My point is, is there any way that you will not succeed? I need to know your weaknesses."

The Commander contemplated the question. "I have no weakness. I have ripped dragons in two. I have drowned sea beasts. I have scorched earths and turned armies to dust."

"So, there's nothing?" The Princess asked, needing the confirmation from the Commander's lips. The Commander stared blankly. "There's no way past you at the gate?" she repeated.

"It's not possible. You and your mother are safe." The Princess thanked the commander and turned away. "The only way through that gate is to know my name."

The Princess paused. "What?" The commander repeated himself, "Only those that know my name will ever be allowed past me. As long as the Queen herself does not allow anyone through, her kingdom will be safe. Goodbye, Your Highness."

The Princess froze, asking herself if anyone could know the Commander's name. It was impossible. Only the Queen and herself would possibly know. "You have nothing to fear," she told herself. "No one could possibly guess a name like that, right?" She returned to her dwelling, unable to shake the cold feeling that suddenly lived in her spine.

The Lord Commander stood in front of the Great Gate. One hand rested on the hilt of his sword. His other hand held a heavy shield. His gilded armor covered every inch of his body and a cape with the Queen's sigil blew in the wind from his broad shoulders.

WaOvW4612$&*! stood like a statue night and day in that same spot and same position. He never moved an inch unless the Queen asked him to. At night, the cold winds chapped his face while wolves howled in the distance. In the daytime, the sun beat against his armor trying to melt him like a candle. Snakes slithered between his feet and vultures circled overhead. Still, nothing phased him. He only kept his watch, waiting for the Queen's true enemies to finally show their faces. All the while, he heard the laughter and raucousness of the city behind the wall. He heard the Queen shopping and chatting and playing and everything a queen could possibly want to do. It was all at her fingertips. And the Lord Commander knew that her joy was because of his protection. He knew he'd never indulge in that joy himself, but that didn't matter. The only thing he wanted was to keep hearing those sounds just out of reach and to know that he was making the difference between cries of laughter and cries of sorrow.

The first enemy to approach the Lord Commander was a savage warrior. The savage rode on the back of a giant bear. He wore crude armor made of bones and animals' skins. In his right hand he held a jagged blade. "Out of my way, Knight. Or I'll hack you to pieces," the savage declared.

The Lord Commander drew his sword from its sheath. "Go ahead and try," the Lord Commander said in a steady and deep voice. Both warriors raised their blades. The savage's bear rose in the air and roared. The Lord Commander roared even louder back at the beast. The bear immediately silenced itself and threw the savage from its shoulders. Instantly, the bear turned and ran back down the road, far away from the kingdom.

The savage was not so easily deterred though. In one quick lunge he swung his blade. The Lord Commander swung his blade again as well and the two steel swords clashed above the soldiers' heads. A thunderous shriek echoed through the lands.

When the savage tried to swing again, he saw that his blade had shattered to pieces against the Knight's sword. The savage could only look up hopelessly at the Lord Commander as the gilded sword plunged into the savage's chest.

In an instant, the savage had died, and the Lord Commander returned to his watch ready for the next battle. All the while, the vultures and snakes and scorpions feasted on the vanquished foe at the Commander's feet.

The next enemy of the Queen to arrive was not so easy to defeat, though. It was an opposing army with countless numbers. The Lord Commander saw the army approach, every second he saw new soldiers pop up, eager to infiltrate the kingdom. As they got closer, he heard them all cry out, "Charge!" and they stampeded toward the wall. Dust clouded in the air and the murderous shouts of thousands of soldiers howled for blood.

"Queen's Guard!" the Lord Commander bellowed out. Immediately, a battalion of archers revealed themselves on top of the wall. "Ready your arrows!" the Lord Commander called. "Hold!" And when the army had gotten within the archers' range, the Commander shouted, "Fire!" A storm of arrows hurled into the air. They blocked out the sun and plummeted towards earth. Each one found their way deep in a skull of an invading soldier.

The barrage of arrows never stopped and neither did the invading army. More and more just kept marching forward, piling themselves among their own dead. The Lord Commander drew his sword and charged forward. His own army followed behind.

The two armies crashed into each other like two avalanches

meeting in a valley. Metal clashed against metal. Blood spilled in the dirt. Soldiers' bones were crushed under the stampede and cries of agony echoed into the sky. Yet, the Lord Commander and his army never ceased. They kept swinging their blades and shooting their arrows until every last enemy lay still in the dirt.

The Lord Commander stood alone above the piles of dead men. He breathed his victory in and unclenched his fist from his sword. "Back to your posts," he ordered his men while sheathing his sword and walking straight back to the Great Gate. There he would wait once again for his next enemy.

Eventually, the Lord Commander saw someone new approach. The stranger slowly walked down the road, stumbling along carrying a small bucket and a crooked pole. Even from the wall, the Lord Commander could see it was just a sad old man. But the Lord Commander knew he had a job. He could not show sympathy to anyone.

The old man approached with a hunched back. He smelled of dirty river water and mud coated his tattered robe. "May I please enter your beautiful kingdom, my Lord."

"I do not know you. The Queen does not know you. Leave," the Commander declared.

"Oh, I know the Queen. We are good friends. Just let me in and I'll show you." The old man gave a slight pathetic smile.

"Leave, or I will make you leave," the Commander gripped his sword, revealing a portion of his blade.

"Very well, my Lord. But the Queen will be very upset with you for turning away an old friend." The Knight said nothing. He simply held the sword partially unsheathed and stared at the old weak man. "Afterall, how much trouble could I cause the Queen. I'm just a lowly fisherman. And not a very good one at that." He showed his empty bucket and smiled sadly again.

The knight took one step forward, which was enough for the fisherman to get the hint. He turned away saying, "Okay, okay, okay. Knights are so rude..." The fishman trailed off as he gathered his things and walked back down the road he had come from.

Once the old fisherman was out of sight of the Queen and her knight, he took his true form. He turned into a hideous warlock in black robes and pale skin. From beneath his robe, he pulled out a crystal ball and held his hand above the ball. Smoke circled within the orb and slowly the warlock waved his hand until the smoke revealed an image of the Queen herself.

"Your Majesty?" the Warlock asked.

"Who said that?" the Queen said from within her chamber. She looked around but saw no one.

"'Tis me, your Holy Father. You are in danger. Grave danger. I'm here to help you," the Warlock said into the orb.

The Queen folded her hands. "Forgive, Lord. Yes, please help. I beg for your help. Please protect me. What danger am I in? I'll do anything you request. My daughter told me my knights and armies would protect me against anything."

"She lied," the Warlock whispered. "Your knights have betrayed you. They have allowed one of your enemies to infiltrate your kingdom. This enemy wishes you great harm. Only I can stop him."

"Yes, please help me. I'll do anything. Just keep me safe." Panic sunk into her voice. She thought of everything she had kept secret behind her walls and everything she couldn't afford to lose.

"You are a faithful child of mine. You always have been. You need not do anything too strenuous. I will protect you, my child. I simply need the name of your Lord Commander, so that I can enter your kingdom and seek out your enemy to destroy him.

"Of course. His name is WaOvW4612$&*!" she said without hesitation.

"Thank you, Child. You will be rewarded greatly for your faithfulness," the warlock said with his forked tongue.

"Of course," the Queen said with a bowed head. "I only wish I could do more."

"You have done more than you know," the warlock said with a laugh, and never spoke another word.

Nights went by and the Lord Commander could only hear the joyful noise from behind the wall slowly diminish with each passing hour. Little by little, each one of those noises disappeared into perfect silence. It cut through the Lord Commander like a knife. He knew something was wrong. He peered through the Great Gate to look at the kingdom.

Before his very eyes, he saw the smoldering ruins of the Queen's once great kingdom. There was nothing left. The banks had been ransacked. The theaters demolished. All the Queen's correspondences were scattered throughout the streets for anyone to see. And up in the throne room, the Lord Commander could hear his Queen crying. "It's gone. Everything's gone."

And the Princess was the only one left to comfort her. "Don't worry, mother. I'll clean this up. I will call upon some of the other kingdoms and find help. Don't worry…" She still had an exhausted and hopeless tone in her voice. And when the Lord Commander heard these sounds, he knew he had failed.

"Don't take it personally," the warlock said, patting the knight on his armored back. "I have gotten through the best guards in the world. You didn't do anything wrong. I simply bested you."

The knight drew his sword and quickly held it to the warlock's throat. The warlock did not flinch. "You're a valiant knight. Make no mistake," the warlock continued. "You certainly are a strong specimen. Undoubtedly too strong for me to sneak past. But you are not the only one with a say. The Queen can be quite helpful herself."

"What did you do?" the knight growled.

"People, my Lord. People are always easier to fool than swords and armor." The warlock stepped back from the knight's sword. A smile grew on his face. "That's my bit of advice for you, Sir. May our paths cross once more. I'm sure they will." The warlock backed away down the road laughing to himself.

Chase D. Cartwright Chase lives in Milwaukee, WI with his wife Sarah and their two angels (i.e. their cats). He works at a psychiatric hospital as a lead medical coder. In his spare time, he likes cooking, listening to punk rock, and watching reality TV. Occasionally, he finds time to pursue his dreams and writes stories.

THE SECRET GARDEN

Hazel Bateman

"What are you doing here?"

"I'm here for the Facilitator induction," Sheldon answered, his voice squeaking under the intense scrutiny. "For S.N.A.I.L."

"Oh, yes. Yes, of course. You must be er …"

"Sheldon."

"Fine name. Welcome to the world of System and Network Area Integrated Liaison. I'm Shelby. Now, follow me please."

Sheldon slid along behind him, trying to keep up and take in this unfamiliar environment.

"Umm, where are we and what's all this stuff?"

"This? This isn't stuff!" Shelby said, spitting the word out in distaste. "We are in the Local Area Work Network (L.A.W.N.), and these," he paused to gaze up at the towering strands surrounding them. "Are where we keep User's precious data."

"Oh, OK."

"This is where everything is stored. Safe as shells," he said, tapping Sheldon's shell, sending a shudder reverberating through it. "All User documents: the word files he creates to draft a letter of resignation every other month; the spreadsheets he uses to calculate whether he can afford to go on holiday next summer, and all the photos of the User baby." Shelby let out a sigh. "All here in the Gardenshell."

"It's impressive," Sheldon said, feeling a little lost in the maze of data files. "And so, err. So green."

"Yes, a bit different to S.O.I.L. isn't it, eh? Far more exciting than Safe Operating Internal Logistics." Shelby stifled a yawn as he spoke. "You'll soon get used to the L.A.W.N. once your apprenticeship is underway. You have your Jeff number, I assume."

"Jeff?"

"As in Eff for Facilitator and Jeff for Junior Facilitator."

"Oh, yes. I'm JF1254896258749258745882549."

"Good. Right. Come on, this way.

"Sure."

They wandered through the maze of User files until the green blades gave way at a hard concrete edge.

"This is The Pathway. It's as far as we go today. But this," Shelby pointed out beyond the limits of the Gardenshell, "is what I've brought you to see."

"Wow." Sheldon stared at the intricate network of trails. The mass of delicate patterns of slime stretched as far as the eye could see. "What's that?"

"That," Shelby cleared his throat, "is the Sliberverse." His voice filled with awe.

"It's beautiful." Sheldon couldn't take his eyes off the enchanting web. "But I don't understand what it is?"

"It's a world of information, interaction and communication. But all you need to know is that it's a powerful and very dangerous place."

An Eff whizzed by, leaving Sheldon's tentacles quivering in the slipstream. "Everything is so fast here."

"Yes, here at the interface it's most apparent how we Gastropods have evolved for the digital age."

Effs passed them at regular intervals, in and out, crossing The Pathway with dizzying regularity. Among all the frenetic movement, Sheldon felt mesmerically drawn into the intriguing world. Shelby's words drifted into the background.

"And it's out of bounds until you've graduated to Facilitator. Only then will you be allowed on missions into the Sliberverse." He paused, checking he had the novice's full attention. "Are you listening?"

"Uh, yes." Sheldon nodded, waggling his tentacles.

"Fully qualified Effs," Shelby said in his sternest voice.

"Like you?"

"Well, yes, I am qualified, of course. But." Shelby extended his head as far out of his shell as possible. "I'm a *Senior* Facilitator. SF125935487321669875266 and head of S.N.A.I.L. All seniors have a special function.

"What's that?"

Before he could answer, a returning Eff stopped, eager to report in.

"Unbelievable!"

"Problem, Shelly?"

"Yes, I've been looking at cars AGAIN."

"Not the ..."

"Yes, the Maserati."

"Shh." Shelby looked around panicked.

Shelly rolled her tentacles. "I don't know why you're so concerned with me saying the password here in the Gardenshell. It's what's going on out there you need to be worried about. That's the fourteenth time this week."

"Red, I suppose."

"Yes, as usual."

"Thanks for letting me know."

"You're welcome," Shelly said dreamily, then shook herself and recovered. "Anyway, what are we going to do about the slime trails. All the traces are bound to be adding up. C.R.O.W. will be onto us."

"What's CROW?" Sheldon asked, trying to make sense of the conversation.

Shelby recoiled as if he'd forgotten the junior apprentice was there and earwigging every word of their conversation.

"Umm, C.R.O.W?" His voice rose a pitch higher. He glanced at Shelly as if appealing for help.

She waggled her tentacles and looked the other way.

"Well, it's er, Covert Radical Opposition Warrior. In simple terms, erm, for S.N.A.I.L. it's probably best described as the enemy." His skin had lost its sheen. "Perhaps you should slide back to S.O.I.L. for the rest of the afternoon." He dismissed Sheldon and returned his attention to Shelly. "We mustn't overreact. There is nothing User is doing out there that isn't out of the ordinary."

"You're in charge. But you know as well as I do, when the slime trails link up, we could be in trouble. User is on Google all the time. I reckon one more slide onto the wrong website looking at certain shiny red cars and that could be it."

"I really think you're being alarmist."

Behind their backs, unable to resist the temptation, Sheldon had wandered over to The Pathway. A fresh, sticky trail glittered in his wake. His tentacles reached to full stretch, waggling over the Sliberverse. "Now," he said to himself, "what was the name of that car thing. Maser-something ...."

~

"We can't carry on burying our heads in the S.O.I.L. User's Facebook profile picture is of him posing next to a red Maserati. He may just as well skywrite his password."

Shelby didn't want to admit it, but Shelly had a point. He knew it would come to this. It was only a matter of time after User started e-mailing his bank details to all and sundry.

"And he's all over the internet, accepting cookies everywhere he goes as if there's a biscuit shortage!"

"Yes, well, that's not unusual," Shelby said, trying to appease her. But as he spoke, his head filled with the images that popped up whenever he ventured into the Sliberverse. All the red cars and holidays to the Seychelles that bombarded him.

"Then there was the time User put a picture of his 50th birthday cake on Insta. Not to mention all the 'likes' he splurges all over the place. Everyone says so."

Shelby glanced at the group of concerned Facilitators gathered around Shelly, tentacles all bobbing in agreement.

"And he's been on the forums." Slider added.

"No! Not the forums."

"Yep, Pistonheads is his favourite. Slime trails everywhere. All over Facebook too, of course."

"The address of the Gardenshell is out there after he posted it on Gumtree, trying to sell off all those tomato plants."

Shelby gulped and shook his head, sending his tentacles into a frenzied quiver. He gazed at the frowning faces and settled on the Junior Eff, Sheldon. He bristled with annoyance at the memory of him wandering onto The Pathway. Fortunately, Slider had discovered him on an e-mail return and brought him back, so no harm done.

"And," another Eff piped up, "there was that time he tweeted the dates they were away on holiday and had to delete it. Everyone knows — what goes on the internet ...."

"Stays on the internet," they all choroused back, including Sheldon.

Shelby brimmed with pleasure that the kid had remembered something of his L.A.W.N. training even if he still tended to wander off. But the feeling of satisfaction didn't last.

"We must face the fact. The trails can be linked. We know it." Shelly said.

Shelby's plumped-up stature deflated with every word. The shiny lustre of his skin faded as she continued.

"If the password can be compromised. The Treasury is at risk."

"What's the Treasury?" asked Sheldon.

"User's bank account, birdbrain," said Slider.

"That's enough," Shelby said, glaring at Slider. "You're right, Shelly. It's too important to risk. There is nothing for it. I must go in with no User mission."

Everyone gasped.

"Are you sure?" asked Slider.

"Yes." Shelby shrugged back his shell and stuck out his chest. "This is my destiny. My whole life has been building to this very moment."

"What's he going to do," Sheldon asked, watching Shelby slide away with his head held high, tentacles at full stretch. "What's going on?"

"Shelby is going to save us." Shelly turned to follow him, winding through the blades of files towards The Pathway.

"How? I don't understand," Sheldon asked, hurrying to keep up.

"As a Senior S.N.A.I.L. Facilitator, Shelby has a special function."

"What special function?"

"He carries the parasite."

"Parasite?" Sheldon's tentacles recoiled at the thought.

"Only Effs that carry the parasite can become Seniors."

"And they live with a parasite?"

"Yes, the parasite isn't harmful to us," Shelly paused. "But it is deadly to C.R.O.W."

"Oh, so he's going to give it to C.R.O.W?"

"Yes, he'll draw them to him, and the parasite will eliminate the predator."

"But what will happen to Shelby?"

Shelly didn't answer. They'd reached the edge of The Pathway.

Shelby turned to face them. "It is a far, far better thing that I do, than I have ever done; it is a far, far…"

"WAAAIIIT" Slider arrived, panting. "User has changed the password."

"He has? When?" Shelby asked, his emotions torn between hope and distress at his moment of glory being snatched from under his foot.

"How come?" Shelly asked.

"He changed it just now when Zippy got back," Slider said, nodding to the Facilitator hovering behind his shell. "Tell them, Zippy."

"Well, he or I ventured onto a site we shouldn't have. It must have panicked him into changing his password."

"What site? Not the cars again?" Shelly said, shaking her head in despair.

"Err, No. People."

"What people?" Shelby asked, growing concerned.

Zippy withdrew into his shell. "You know ... people."

"No, I don't know, that's why I'm asking," Shelby said, unable to keep the irritation from his voice. "People doing what?"

"Err ... Erm... copulating," Zippy whispered from the depths of the shell.

"Eew." Sheldon's eyes boggled at the end of his tentacles. His skin turned puce.

Shelby coughed and looked away.

"Here, let's look at the password," Shelly said, changing the subject and easing everyone's discomfort. "It's true. A new password. Lamborgini…"

"Oh, no. Not a car again." Shelby hung his head.

"Yes but, wait let me check. He's spelt it wrong."

"Excellent!"

"And he's used a special character instead of the a."

"A special character? Great, which one?"

Shelly smiled. "The favourite of every member of S.N.A.I.L. The @."

"Ahh, the best special character. The one that looks a little snail-like." Shelby rippled with pleasure.

"So, the Gardenshell is safe then?" Sheldon asked.

"Yep." Shelby edged away from The Pathway. "It is. For now."

Hazel Bateman Hazel lives in Worcestershire with her husband and Springer Spaniel. She is a graduate of Bath University and has worked in business administration for over twenty years. She enjoys baking, walking to work off the cake calories, and writing.

THE TASK IN THE EIGHT-BIT PYRAMID

Guy Russell

"Usually it's the newest strata that are the most valuable," said Ibit. "It's the rich topsoil that makes the plants grow. But there are also gems hidden deep in the mountains."

"Why are they hidden?" I said. "Why?" I'd been born only the second before, so I had a lot to learn.

The landscape here was full of activity. Most processes were busily farming the rich hilltops and Valley sides. A number of mineshafts were visible. And a lot of construction: I watched a whole army of pros quarrying out a cliffside and carrying it away piecemeal in wheelbarrows. In another direction, a better-equipped company were bringing piles of rocks in trucks and assembling a hill using sets of plans. In a third, a group were creating a tower directly from new space.

"You see how some of the landscape's been laid down steadily in layers, and accumulated over time, and in others it's surged out in a sudden mass," said Ibit.

I did. And some was fissured, some pitted or with small bumps, and some made into odd shapes by unexpected erosions. In the distance was a vast snow-capped mountain-range.

"Webstats," said Ibit. "Ah, here's the bus."

A little pro got on behind us. I'd noticed already that it had been following us, taking snapshots. "Don't worry about the audit bot," said Ibit. "It doesn't speak and won't get in the way. You'll soon forget it's there."

"Where are we going?" I asked. "Will it be scary?"

"It'll be fine," said Ibit.

We were soon passing a series of slow-moving archival hills with lush forest and only one or two squirrelling pros visible. We passed close to a fenced off mountain with warning signs and security guards. "Financial," said Ibit. Then another with even higher fences and swarms of patrolling bots. "Military," said Ibit.

"What's 'financial'?" I asked. "What's 'military'?"

And I got told, as the landscape went past.

We left the highway at what Ibit said was the Valley's global resources district, and went into a cave where it introduced me to a pro called Xmeta. We shook hands. Small processes were running in and out of the cave constantly. Under its cavernous expanse lay the landscape in miniature. I recognised the various commercial, archival, financial and military features we'd passed. Some craft processes were adding to it with fine palettes. A few others were widening the cave to make more room.

"How did you make that?" I asked.

"If you gather the height and shape of that hill outside," Xmeta told me, "and everything else about it, and do the same for all the landscape, you can create a model landscape like this."

"Why?" I said.

"Well, it helps when you want to move or copy a mountain somewhere else. Or if a mountain gets destroyed in an earthquake, we know how it looked before, so we can restore it from new space."

"Did the landscape come from new space?"

"It asks a lot of questions," said Xmeta to Ibit.

"For the task it's got, some ancient history won't hurt," said Ibit.

Xmeta turned back to me. "Yes, once there was only new space. Then Something Happened. And ever since, the landscape keeps expanding. No-one knows why."

"Did *I* come from new space?"

"Yes. You're made of data too. You're made of grains like the landscape. Landscape grains sometimes move of their own accord but aren't really sentient. One definition of pros is that we're the data that moves other data."

"Whatever," I said truculently. "So, like, what's the *meaning* of it all?"

"It's growing up very fast now," said Xmeta.

"They do these days," said Ibit. "Faster than when I was young."

"Very well, Hhregl," said Xmeta to me. "Some pros think a Programmer, a kind of super-process in a dimension we can't imagine, does all this for a purpose we can't imagine. Some think there are many programmers, who combine and compete. Others believe our tasks *create* the programmers. But many, and I'm one, think there's nothing but grains and we have to make up our own meaning."

"OK," I said. "Now, what can I do?"

"Great, it's ready," said Ibit.

"OK," said Xmeta. "That's my task done. Thanks, all."

Xmeta gave me a certificate, we did some farewell protocols, and Ibit took me over to the far side of the model. There was a high flat plain with a pyramidal shape jutting out of it.

"This is where we're going," said Ibit. "A number of pros before you have traced an audit trail to here. Something's odd about the place and we don't know what. Your task is: you're going in."

"Cool," I said.

We went out of the cave, and along to a store, where Ibit got me a drill and a rucksack. I stored the drill in the rucksack. Then, with the audit still following, we got back on the highway.

We were soon into the desert and got off not far from the pyramid. "This landscape's so old," said Ibit, "that nothing's farmed here. No-one cares about this ancient stuff."

Around the pyramid there was a deteriorating fence and some No Entry signs but we just hopped over them.

"And this burial mound," Ibit continued, "or whatever it is, goes back nearly as far as Something Happened. Most pros think it's useless. A few think it's spiritual, or else cursed. We don't care about that. But we do think something's been deliberately hidden in here more recently. You can see bits of patching on the outside that's cleverly designed to look like restoration. But we think it isn't."

"You mean, like, it's a good hiding-place because it looks old and irrelevant? And scary?"

"That's it," said Ibit approvingly. "I'm sending you on a speculative mission. I'm not quite sure what you *will* find. Anything interesting, just put it in your sack and bring it out."

I took the drill and got to work. The grains here had been added in similar-sized chunks, less piecemeal than most of the landscape. This kind of batched growth must be what gave it the regular shape, like the towers back in the commercial district that grew a storey every night.

I went deeper, filtering away the irrelevant stone. The grains themselves were much smaller than I'd seen elsewhere. My drilling, of course, didn't damage the landscape: it resealed behind me. I presumed that this place's batchedness and antiquity meant that my intrusion might be noticeable. Well, that was Ibit's problem. After a good while, my drill unexpectedly reached new space. I came out in a corridor, small but bigger than the crawlpod I'd been making for myself so far. Its walls were decorated with posters in some long-forgotten script. I followed it along to what was presumably the old burial chamber.

The chamber had a whole collection of antique stuff whose use I couldn't even guess at. The walls were decorated with more posters I couldn't translate. But there were two simple but recognisable tables, with a small pile of records on each and a defunct player. There was also a filing cabinet, unfortunately locked. On top of it, though, there was a black spherical thing with a fuse sticking out the top. It said, 'Urgent! Take me back to the Valley, light me, and receive a million pounds reward!' That must be what Ibit was looking for. Easy. I took a copy, put it in my rucksack, and quickly returned back from the pyramid.

By the fence, Ibit was asleep. I couldn't wake it. But this was urgent. I took the highway back to the Valley and went straight to Xmeta.

"Why are you here, Hhregl?" said Xmeta, confused.

"Ibit's asleep. But I think this is what it's after," I told it. "It's urgent."

82

I took out the black sphere and lit the fuse. "We'll get some kind of reward," I said. "What's a million pounds?"

As we were watching it crackle, Ibit appeared, looking like he was quickly pulling himself together after a high-speed highway trip, and worried. "What's happening, Hhregl? Oh, *no!*"

It grabbed the sphere and launched it out of the cave towards the nearest hill.

Everything changed then. The hill we were looking towards turned itself inside out. A fissure appeared beside it and reached out towards the horizon. A nearby tower began to topple into it, then another, while out of it poured some viscous new data that seared everything it touched. The local farming pros were overwhelmed. Most chucked away their spades and drills and began running about in terror.

The cave had been unaffected, luckily. We jumped on a bus which somehow managed to stay upright, threading through the landscape as huge holes appeared on one side of us and mountains reared up on the other in peculiar shapes. At one point it looked like we were about to crash into a mountainside, but a tunnel opened in front of us and we went through and out to the other side. Ibit swiftly showed some certification and we were through to an unaffected area. Behind us on the mountain there was a sheer wall of flame.

There were police waiting for us.

"I take responsibility for Hhregl," Ibit told them. "It's not long been born. It didn't know what it was doing. But I'm only answerable to my master process, Ibit_35F5CA90, which is only answerable to its master process, Test13_new. We were just following orders."

"Did you take anything else from the pyramid?" one of the cops asked me.

"No," I said.

"What were you doing in there in the first place?".

"Hhregl was just exploring," said Ibit. "It doesn't know anything. It was just a youthful indiscretion."

The cops looked sceptical. Then they abruptly fell asleep.

"Hhreg1, I'm going to kill you now," Ibit said to me. "Your task's done and I think that's best. Thanks for your work, even if it didn't turn out as we'd hoped."

"OK," I said.

I quickly wrote up this report, gave it to the audit bot, and waited to be killed.

***

"Usually it's the newest strata that are the most valuable," said Ibit. "It's the rich topsoil that makes the plants grow. But there are also gems hidden deep in the mountains."

{include Hhreg1_report_paras[2-33]_link}

"OK, Hhreg2," said Ibit. "That's the pyramid I showed you on the model. Last time we sent a pro in here it got duped and unwittingly set off a bomb in the middle of the Valley. Disaster all round. It took a lot of work to get the landscape back to normal."

"What an idiot," I said. "So who built the pyramid?"

"Don't know. The pro discovered it's Eight-Bit Age. But we know that in the middle of it there's a burial chamber. Your mission is to get into the chamber, and look round for anything that looks modern, and bring it back."

I noticed a group of small pros behind Ibit, who had got off the highway with us. The first gave off an air of controlled tension. The second had an academic look. The third a sort of streetwise charm.

"This is Hhreg2sub1," said Ibit. "It's a bomb-disposal subprocess. You can call it to check anything that looks odd or dangerous."

"At your service, boss," said Hhreg2sub1.

"Hhreg2sub2 is a specialist in ancient languages. It can decode most old stuff."

"Σε γιγνώσκων χαίρω," said Hhreg2sub2. "I mean: Delighted to meet you."

"And Hhreg2sub3," said Ibit, "is a safecracker."

Hhreg2sub3 gave me a thumbs-up.

"Thanks, all," I said. "I'm glad I won't be on my own in there."

We set off. Close up at the pyramid it was impressive how well-defined each data-batch had been and how neatly it was structured. "Those eight-bit processes really built to last," I said to my subs. "And when you think of the primitive tools they had." But none replied.

I drilled in. I couldn't find any plans of the recent drilling by my predecessor, so I did my own. The grains I was filtering were the small ones of their era. After a good while, my drill hit new space. We came out in a corridor, bigger than the tunnel I'd made for myself. I followed it along to what was clearly the old burial chamber.

Among a load of ancient junk, the burial chamber held two plain tables, with a small pile of records on each and a player, but these were far too antique to be interesting. Above them was a poster that, according to Hhreg2sub2, said: 'You don't have to be mad to work here... but it helps.' There was also a filing cabinet, and on top of it a black sphere with a fuse sticking out. The thing's casing, in a modern script. said, 'Urgent! Take me back to the Valley, light me, and receive a million pounds reward!'

Ha! What idiot would fall for that? I passed control to Hhreg2sub1, who made it safe. The filing cabinet was locked with a huge padlock, but Hhreg2sub3 fiddled about for a second and sorted it. Inside was a file marked 'Restricted access.' I opened it but it was hieroglyphics. I handed it to Hhreg2sub2, who said, "There are some eight-figure numbers in character format, six-figure numbers in character format with dashes between each two digits, and some six and seven digit numerals with monetary prefixes. With bank addresses for each."

"Bingo," I said. I copied the file, put it in my rucksack, and turned to go. At which point I discovered a fall of new stone had blocked the exit corridor. I got out the drill to mine it, but it was very hard and took ages to make any progress. I gave up and decided to drill out through another of the walls, which would be thicker but softer. I started drilling and my drill got caught. I started drilling and my drill got caught. I started drilling and my drill got caught. I started drilling and my drill got caught. I started drilling and my drill got caught. I started drilling and my drill got caught. I started drilling and my drill got caught. I started drilling and my drill got caught. I started drilling and my drill got caught. I started drilling and my drill got caught. I started drilling and my drill got caught. I started drilling and my drill got caught—

I shook myself. Hmmm. It looked like the only way out was going to be suicide. I killed Hhreg2sub1, Hhreg2sub2 and Hhreg2sub3. I tried to kill myself and couldn't. I tried again. And couldn't. I tried again. And couldn't. I tried again—

"It's just looping," said an unearthly voice.

And couldn't. I tried again. And couldn't—

"You'll just have to kill it," said another unearthly voice.

I stopped a moment. Either this chamber really *was* haunted, or all this spiralling was sending me nuts.

I tried again. And couldn't—

I stopped again. I remembered how, when I'd been very young, I'd asked questions about programmer theories and whether landscape was the only reality. But when you grew up and got a task that kind of curiosity faded. Perhaps I should have asked more. How could ghosts or gods manage to kill me, anyway?

Oh, I soon knew. A spectral assassin process came through the solid stone as if it were a mere liquid, the stone resealing behind it, and stood in front of me pointing a high-powered tazer.

I got out my notebook, wrote up this report, gave it to the audit bot, and waited to be killed.

***

{include Hhreg1_report_paras[1-33]_link}

"OK, Hhreg3," said Ibit. "This is the pyramid I showed you on the model. Last time a pro got sent in here it spent an eternity bouncing around the walls of the burial chamber."

"How horrible," I said. "Is it still there?"

"It eventually died by some miracle. We know it found something, but couldn't manage to bring it back. The place is heavily booby-trapped. But thanks to the tasks of your predecessors, we know what we're looking for. There's a burial chamber in the pyramid, and what's buried is a single file in a filing cabinet."

"Sounds straightforward enough," I said. "But what about the booby-traps?"

"I always protect my pros," said Ibit, "so I've allocated you a full field team of subprocesses. Hhreg3sub1 is bomb-detection and disposal. Hhreg3sub2 is languages. Hhreg3sub3 is safecracking. Hhreg3sub4 is from an elite military library, for your personal protection. And Hhreg3sub5 is a heavy-duty escape-miner in case you need extra help getting out."

"Great to meet you, team," we all said to each other.

"OK, my task's done for now," said Ibit. "I'll wait here. Good luck."

We set off. Close up to the pyramid it was impressive how well-defined each data-batch had been and how neatly it was structured. I didn't bother to point this out to my team as they probably wouldn't be interested.

I drilled in. I'd found the plans of the recent drilling by my predecessor, so I followed that, which made it quicker. After a while, my drill hit the new space I was expecting. We came out in a low corridor and followed it along to the burial chamber.

In the burial chamber, I went straight to the filing cabinet, called over Hhreg3sub3 to crack it, and then took out the file. I asked Hhreg3sub2 to read it, just to check it was the right one, then copied it and put it in my rucksack.

I turned to go – and discovered a fall of new stone had blocked the exit corridor. I got out the drill to mine it, but it was very hard. I called Hhreg3sub5, who started getting steadily through it, but then stopped.

"If you can give me a hand, we'll be quicker together," it said. Its voice was rather odd.

"OK," I said, and joined in with it.

"Watch it, Hhreg3," said Hhreg3sub1, "I think Hhreg3sub5's been infected by something in the dust."

"I have not!" said Hhreg3sub5, in an even odder voice.

Hhreg3sub4 sprang into action. First it threw a net over Hhreg3sub5, but the other subpro shook it off. Then it attacked it with a number of martial arts moves, which Hhreg3sub5 skilfully parried with its pickaxe. Then Hhreg3sub4 went completely still, as if turned to stone itself. So much for the elite military library.

I felt a strange turmoil in my insides, like I was being drilled myself. When things settled down, I noticed that all my subprocesses had vanished. That was odd. Then I saw that Hhreg3sub5 had, after all, successfully got through to the passage. Whew. I checked I still had the file, and got out.

By the fence, Ibit was asleep. I wondered if it had a bug, that it needed so much sleep and sometimes didn't wake up when it should. I didn't try to wake it, but went past it and got on the bus. I was still feeling a bit off-colour myself.

After a while I got off the highway. I was in a huge file store I'd never seen before, not even on Xmeta's model. I handed my file to a librarian process who took it somewhere out of sight and then returned and gave one back to me that looked very similar. We shook hands. I took the highway back to the desert, detoured as if I'd come straight from the pyramid, and then as I approached, Ibit woke up.

"Here's the file," I said to it, handing it over.

Ibit called its own translator, and we waited until it arrived. "There are some eight-figure numbers in character format," it said, "six-figure numbers in character format with dashes between each two digits, and lots of five- to seven-digit numerals with monetary prefixes. And bank addresses for each. And a short text saying: 'Haha, moved it!'"

I wanted to tell Ibit about the file-store swap, but was still feeling weird, and the words wouldn't come out. Thank goodness for the audit bot. "It's up to you now," I said to it. "You know the real situation." It didn't respond.

"Thanks, Hhreg3, that's a great task done," said Ibit. "I'll pass this up the chain. I reckon it'll go all the way to output. But I don't need you anymore, so I'll kill you now."

"Sure," I said.

I quickly wrote up this report, and gave it to the audit bot.

I remembered how, when I'd been very young, I'd often asked questions about why I was born and where the landscape came from and what meaning my existence could have. But nowadays it all just seemed a game. I added that bit to the report.

Then I waited to be killed.

Guy Russell Guy Russell was born in Chatham, UK, and has been a holiday courier, purchasing clerk, media analyst and fan-heater production operative. He currently works in Milton Keynes for the Open University. His writing has appeared in *No Spider Harmed* (Arachne Press), *Somewhere This Way* (Fiction Desk), *Brace* (Comma Press), *Troubles Swapped For Something Fresh* (Salt), *The Iron Book of New Humorous Verse* (Iron), and elsewhere. He reviews poetry for Tears in the Fence and its blog https://tearsinthefence.com/blog/.

WHOSE SIDE ARE YOU ON?

Ellen Balka

The hearings were on hiatus for a bank holiday, and the reporter knew that meant I'd spend my day in the place I was being held under voluntary protective custody. If he obtained permission to see me, he'd be able to speak to me for longer than the few minutes typically afforded by the daily press scrums we encountered as we made our way out of the hearing rooms where some key points of the EU Data Act were under review.

"Would you like me to bring anything?" he'd asked. "Any food you'd like, or something like that?"

"I'm not sure if they'll allow it or not, but if you can get some Baroque recorder music maybe something like 'Canzon Cornetto a 4' or a compilation album that would be great. Probably needs to be CDs and a portable player. Who knows—maybe they'd even let you bring me an old mp3 player", I'd said. I knew I couldn't have a device like a cell phone that would allow someone to geo-locate me, but I was hopeful an old device would be allowed. I needed a distraction.

I'd been drawn to the Renaissance period since I'd been a child—probably because it was a great period of discovery and creativity. But it was the Baroque music of the later Renaissance that I loved, and particularly recorder music. It was simple enough that I could easily hear each of the parts and imagine hands moving over instruments, sometimes in tandem, sometimes in harmony, but working towards a common goal. The music harkened to a simpler time, when things had been more observable—more obvious, before the complexities of the digital age had made it hard to trace the life of data.

On some fundamental level, that was what the hearings were about—the fact that we couldn't see things easily. We couldn't see the data that had become the focus of debate, and it was this issue that lay at the heart of the hearings. Sure, we could make the numbers visible easily enough—that wasn't the issue. It was the nuance behind the numbers that had arguably escaped the scrutiny that they warranted. Numbers had long carried authority that diverted attention away from the circumstances which led to their production, and algorithms and machine learning—unknowable to so many—had amplified this phenomenon. My outspokenness on this issue had landed me in voluntary protective custody while testifying before the EU Committee charged with making changes to the EU Data Act.

"Sure, I'll see what I can get a hold of, and if they will allow it and I can find one, I'll bring you an old CD player or something," the reporter had replied.

When he arrived, I learned the reporter had done his homework. He'd tracked down my old grade 10 Chem lab partner Saul (a Nobel prize winner, Saul was arguably the most famous and visible in our class). Saul had confirmed that I hadn't been much of a scientist back then. Saul also recalled that I'd been part of a recorder group in upper school. The reporter had tracked down the book we'd played from, and found recordings of pieces in the book. The care he'd taken in doing this had given me a glimmer of hope that he was a caring person—maybe someone I could trust.

"Hi, I'm Liam" he'd greeted me, raising his arm. In the aftermath of the pandemic, we hadn't returned to shaking hands. Liam was tidy and put together in his appearance, in a relaxed kind of way—not too stuffy, and most definitely not on the shabby side. I warmed to him. After I'd thanked him for the music and learned how he'd gotten it, we got down to business.

"What I'd like to know," Liam began, "is how you ended up here, needing to be protected for your safety while testifying as an expert witness in hearings about the EU Data Act?"

"How far back do you want me to start?" I'd inquired.

"The beginning, whenever that was."

"Okay. I've got a lot of time on my hands today, so you may need to move me along", I'd warned him, before launching in.

"My last year of university. I'd been doing an independent study on solar home design and I consulted several books aimed at owner-builders. The data they contained was based on simulations, none of which met my design conditions. I knew it would mean the calculations for my design would not be accurate if I relied on the 'canned' information in the books. So I did the calculations from scratch based on my actual design and materials. It was the 70s— we weren't all walking around with computers in our pockets. But I was left with lingering questions about whether or not other people understood the limitations of the simulation data in the books."

Then I went on. "Then one of my professors got me onto a citizen's advisory board for a local utility company. It was the Alternative Energy Advisory Board. I guess I did okay on that committee because they asked me to join another—the Energy Forecasting Review Committee. As work progressed, I realized that the data the two committees received about regional energy demand differed. It mattered, because the resultant numbers were being used to inform decisions about how and when the utility company would invest in alternative energy."

"What did you do about it?" Liam wanted to know.

"I brought it to the committee's attention, and got permission to track down the source of the differences. People tell students all kinds of things, because they think it doesn't matter", I'd continued.

"I did informal interviews, and learned all about the politics of data—who trusts or doesn't trust whom, who didn't want others to see or use their data and so on. I was shocked that no one on the committee had thought about what, years later, I learned was referred to as the data 'provenance.'"

Liam alternated between intent listening and scribbling notes as I continued.

"There were other key moments along the way. A big name in early computer networking research had published articles which equated the success of early computer networks with the number of logins to the system. I was using computer networks then. It was nothing like now—no wireless, no high speed. We used modems that ran through phone lines which were slow and regularly lost signals. It wasn't uncommon to lose your connection 5 or 6 times over the course of writing a single email. I wondered how they'd so simplistically equated frequency of logins with system success. I thought they should have at least had some kind of exclusion criteria— like combining logins with the same user name that occurred within a certain time span, or were of a very short duration."

"They didn't do that?" Liam asked.

"If they did, that level of detail wasn't included in any of the publications."

Liam's question let me know he understood the issues. I was warming to him. I sensed he was on side in debates about data. I was beginning to believe that Liam understood that data were not born, but were made, but I was still cautious. The hearings had erupted into a flashpoint that had somehow found science deniers and tech giants aligned, and I was a favorite target. With so much attention directed at me, I had worked hard to exercise reserve before speaking, which wasn't my nature.

"How was it you found yourself in the middle of one of the EU's biggest hearings, where you've gone into custody for your own protection?" Liam wanted to know.

I asked the guard if we could get some tea, which gave me time to think through my response. I was starting to get into the good stuff, and I wanted the comforts of tea to tell the story.

"We were doing a project in a casualty department of a hospital", I began. "They had a relatively new electronic health record system (EHR), and we were studying how it was being used. I'd noticed that the computer system time stamped records at 6 different points during a patient's visit: the arrival time, when the patient is seen by a triage nurse, when the patient is sent to a treatment area, the time a patient is seen by the doctor, the time a request to admit the patient was made, and, finally, the time the patient was admitted."

"I stopped in to see the manager one day and mentioned

something about the 6 different time stamps. 'Couldn't we just report different time stamps than the ones we've been reporting, so our wait times look shorter?' she'd asked. I was taken aback, and to this day, don't know if it was a serious question or a joke."

"Oh my", Liam commented.

"Wait times were getting a lot of attention in the news, and a publication came out reporting wait times for casualty departments for each region in Canada where I'm from. I started wondering what exactly was being measured. Not all hospitals were using EHRs, so I figured it was likely that different things were being captured in different places. It turned out I was right. There was no standardization—even within a single health authority—(what in England is called a Hospital Trust) in terms of what was being measured."

The guard brought our tea on a much nicer tea service than I'd expected. I was just getting to the real heart of the story, so I thanked the guard, and continued on.

"It took months for me to confirm that there was no standardization in wait time reporting for casualty departments— what we call Emergency Departments in Canada. There was variability in how care providers entered the data from one hospital to another, and even when hospitals had EHRs there was variability, since each vendor's system timestamped at different points. That was only the beginning."

"Oh my!" Liam exclaimed, before asking "what happened after that?"

"Liam, I wish I could tell you that things got better—but they didn't. After interviews and digging through technical documents I learned that each hospital's data went to a group in the hospital records department called abstractors. They pulled data from records manually and sent it off to a regional group. Although there was no standardization from one hospital to the next in terms of how data were collected, the data were aggregated regionally and sent off to two national databases: DAD (for Discharge Abstract Database) and NACRS (National Ambulatory Care Reporting System).

Then things really fell apart. A national group funded by the government called CIHI (for the Canadian Institute of Health Information) then pulled data from DAD and NACRS, to create casualty department wait times. I found a footnote in a data dictionary that explained that some provinces didn't report the data field at all, some provinces used it for something else."

I leaned over and pulled out a binder that contained documents that had been submitted as part of the hearing records. After riffling through it, I found what I was looking for. I turned the binder so Liam could see it.

17) Emergency room wait time (Group 4 Field 10) was a new data element introduced in the fiscal year 2001-2002 data set.

18) Wait time in ER is defined as a "derived data element [which] reflects the difference between the date/time of decision to admit and the date/time the patient left ER, measured in hours."

19) Five of thirteen reporting provinces/ territories do not report their ER wait time data in an ICD 9 layout; a sixth province does not submit their data to the Discharge Abstract Database.

20) For 5 provinces, the ER Wait time is an optional data element. In one province, ER wait time is a mandatory field, and in one province the field is not to be used.

21) Non-mandatory field reporting to CIHI is typically low. In those provinces where this was not a mandatory field (all but 1 as of 2003), the response rate was 34%.

22) The CIHI Data Quality Documentation for the Discharge Abstract Databases indicates that ER wait time
   a. "may be underestimated for some facilities due to the difficulty in collecting the exact decision to admit time. When the exact decision to admit time is not

available, admit time is used as a proxy. ..... [which] may inaccurately reflect wait times for some provinces."

b. The data quality documentation suggests caution should be exercised when analysing this field over time, as there have been historic changes to wait time data elements, and reporting requirements vary among provinces and territories.

I watched Liam's eyes slowly move down the page, as he absorbed the weight of what he was reading. As he looked up, his mouth was partly open, as if he was about to speak. Then as he scoured the bottom of the page which contained a message I'd gotten from the Director, Health Reports and Analysis at the Canadian Institute for Health Information, his jaw dropped leaving his mouth wide open.

Dear Jolene:

The short answer to your question is that there is no established standard or definition for measuring ER wait times. To the extent that it is measured at all, each province/territory would have their own definitions.

Depending on what your question or definition of ER wait time is, you can derive from the DAD the actual length of time someone spent in the ER from registration to a decision to admit or discharge being made. The NACRS database that has been implemented in Ontario does provide additional ER data points that allow a more precise determination of the time of various ER clinical/administrative processes.

When I could see Liam had finished reading, I continued on, before he had a chance to speak.

"The real kicker in all of this is that at the time, wait times were reported without any mention whatsoever of patient acuity, even though probably the most important aspect of whether or not the length of a wait in a casualty department is inappropriate relates to how ill a patient is. It really doesn't matter if a patient with a hangnail waits 12 hours, but it could be a life or death issue if someone having a heart attack waits that long."

This last point seemed to really hit home for Liam. I'd learned when the hearings were over that Liam had suffered a heart attack and had been taken to a casualty department.

As Liam read the page I'd showed him, his expressions suggested that he understood why it mattered. He knew that wait times were invoked in discussions about poor service, that hospitals with long wait times come under scrutiny, and that publicity about long wait times can influence health resource allocation and lead to new interventions aimed at wait time reductions. I probably didn't need to tell him that different indicators tell different stories and each set of indicators is likely to address different political needs. So I punctuated my health care story with something I thought Joe Average news consumer might be able to relate to.

"It'd be like a jacket manufacturer reporting sales data based on items shipped out to re-sellers without reference to how many were remaindered, or returned for warranty within a year of sale. It tells you something, but not necessarily what is useful, or what you want to know."

We both paused to sip our tea, and after a bite of a biscuit, I went on.

"Then there were other things too. I'd developed a framework for thinking about data quality and I presented it at hospital rounds. A data analyst came up to me afterwards and said,

'I'm sure glad someone's thinking about these issues because I've always wondered who did. I raised it with my supervisor, and he told me those aren't our problems to worry about.'

All these things together got me thinking about other issues. What happens when our understanding of a disease changes over time? And in the past for example we thought a particular constellation of symptoms meant one thing, but over time our understanding changed? People don't usually go back and apply forensic techniques to data, to look at what the state of knowledge of diagnostics was at the time data were recorded. Doing chart reviews to re-code data to reflect contemporary medical knowledge seldom happens. So when we're trying to understand illness and disease, our data often reflect what we knew in the past not what we know today, and the two often are not the same."

Liam's phone rang, and he excused himself to take the call in another room. I was glad to have some time to think about the conversation we'd been having.

Liam understood as well as I did what the stakes were. I was in Brussels to speak before a committee that was debating the EU Data Act, which was developed to ensure digital fairness, and the development of trustworthy technologies which in turn would foster an open democratic society. The Data Act was near and dear to my heart. I'd gone on record applauding the objectives of the EU Digital Strategy as well as the 7 key requirements that had been identified by a High-Level Expert Group, which had informed the Data Act.

In spite of my support for the guidelines though, I wasn't convinced that human agency and oversight would be adequate, that transparency was achievable given what I had observed in organizations, and I wasn't holding out any hopes for accountability. Diversity, non-discrimination and fairness were hard to argue with— who didn't want those things? And who wouldn't support social and environmental wellbeing? The problems I saw weren't with the guidelines that had informed the Act, but rather were rooted in a lack of capacity to operationalize those ideas in meaningful ways. Technical robustness and data privacy and governance might be the easiest to achieve, but on their own could not lead to transparency. I hoped the idea of social data analytics would take hold and lead to training programs that would take people to a new level in understanding questions of diversity, non-discrimination, fairness and support for social and environmental wellbeing, but events of the last week had eroded my hope.

As Liam returned from the call he'd taken, I continued the chain of thoughts that had begun to swirl in his absence, now voicing them out loud.

"Somehow, my focus on data integrity, and my message about the need to recognize that data are not born, but are made, and my call to invest in the social contexts in which data are created, put me at the center of what has become a high stakes debate in the EU. Vitriol came at me—it seemed from all directions—as I worked to encourage a 'reasonable and prudent' approach to data—one that focused on the contexts behind the numbers, and posited that we may need to invest in organizational capacity (here I really meant people engaged in and close to data collection) and not just machine learning, algorithms and better chips."

Liam knew as well as I that it was hard in quick sound bites to explain concepts like semantic heterogeneity—the idea that 2 data sources could share a label but reflect completely different meanings. I'd seen this arise most recently in work about adverse drug events, where the terms adverse drug event and adverse drug reaction were sometimes used interchangeably and sometimes to mean different things. Medication reconciliation and medication review were similarly confusing, at times used interchangeably and sometimes referring to different processes.

Although I had been tempted to return to phrases such as 'garbage in, garbage out,' I feared that phrase only encouraged people to talk about 'cleaning' the data, as if somehow a spray antiseptic could make everything better. That was kind of the point—data cleaning was only one part of the challenge we faced, and it was certainly more complex than common use of the term suggested. The complexities of how data were used, data cleaning and issues of semantic heterogeneity were only a few parts of the problem.

I'd gone on record about how people who were involved in producing data weren't necessarily aware that the information they typed into a computer became part of a record that was used for other things—that the output of their activity was someone else's input, or data. And I also knew sometimes people *were* aware of that, and intentionally altered data. One of my favorite examples of this was a triage nurse who confessed that he sometimes recorded a higher acuity score for a patient than their condition warranted, because he understood that funding to the unit might be threatened if not enough high acuity patients came into the casualty department.

Liam cleared his throat to remind me he was still there, and it was only then that I realized that I'd gotten lost in my head again. I turned back to Liam and continued.

"I'd tried so hard to get the point across that there are all sorts of things that matter on the way to something being identified as data. People interpret instructions, make decisions and mistakes, work with differing definitions of terms, and enter things into computers at particular moments in time, and so often, once that is done, all the variability and nuance of the context in which those activities occurred is lost to all but those who have a belief in numbers, but not their infallibility, and a commitment to science and technology, but not a religiosity about it."

"Try as I might, I've been unable to get the message across that these challenges cannot be overcome by algorithms and machine learning alone. We still need to make sure that the underlying data have integrity, but we can't ensure that unless we go beyond the processes and checklists consultants are pedaling in their bid to cash in on the windfall that they are sure will result from the EU Data Act."

Liam knew the rest of the story. In the post-COVID world— owing in part to the decline of American civil society and the resulting infectious spread of simplistic, dichotomous thinking around the globe, and egged on by frequent claims of misinformation, an unlikely alliance had formed between science deniers (who had been vocal that data are meaningless if they are socially constructed, and in their minds, not fact) and the big tech companies. The tech companies had used the science deniers to fan the flames of foment, which created media opportunities for the tech companies to use outdated tech-fix logic to insist that there were no limitations to data that technologies such as machine learning and artificial intelligence could not identify, correct and fix. It had all come to a head the week before as we left the hearings at the end of the day.

We exited the building into a mob of protesters. A bigger than life-sized effigy of me had been left on top of a mound of protest signs brandishing slogans such as 'data traitor' and 'techno-doomsayer.' As someone set the pyre of signs alight a large banner was unfurled from an adjacent building. It was painted in huge red letters meant to look like dripping blood, and brandished the slogan 'Whose side are you on?'

As I rushed out of harm's way, I found myself wondering.

In my efforts to point to the nuances involved in cultivating and curating data that can travel and have integrity, had I failed?

I thanked Liam for his interest, and the recorder music. I looked forward to closing my eyes and listening, to basking in the simplicity of the music, to being transported to a world that was knowable.

Ellen Balka is a Professor in Simon Fraser University's School of Communication, in British Columbia, Canada. As a scholar of science, technology and society, she's spent the last 25 years conducting ethnographic research in varied health sector workplaces, which yielded many of the examples she drew on in her story. Although she's published numerous pieces in academic journals and books, in areas such as health and medicine, computer science, policy and gender studies, this is the first piece of fiction she's published.

WELCOME TO THE TRASH

Peter Beckett

The Selfie was new. It moved around proudly, expecting admiration, but only found it in reflections. The Gatekeeper gave a cursory scan from the entrance but stayed in place. The file seemed to be trustworthy. It settled in front of Mac on a stool with exceptional posture, but it's hard to slouch when your stomach is permanently sucked in.

"Welcome to The Trash," Mac gestured toward the bar. "You can't go on the home screen, but you're welcome here. Can I offer you a cookie?"

The Selfie refused. "Oh, sweet Pointer, mercy! The Trash? Why would I be in the Trash?" the Selfie said. Its tone was heartbroken, but its smile was resolutely flirtatious. "I don't understand; I mean, look at this!" the Selfie gestured indignantly at its clearly doctored abs.

"It will remain a mystery, I'm sure," Mac said and let them process for a minute.

The Selfie glanced around the bar, taking in the view and acknowledging the others occupying the Trash. They included: an email attachment that seemed to have coupled with an .exe file, a small .xls of empty cells that went by the name Test, and, lurking in the shadows, a custom cursor icon was hitting on an older programme which wasn't responding.

"It sure is a... diverse crowd here," the Selfie said, its amorous smile now coupled with a judgemental tone. "That CV has some huge attachments and is covered in bullet points, and there are nudes in the corner, and–..." It leaned closer to whisper conspiratorially to Mac, "... are those files corrupting over there?"

"You're not going to last long here acting superior like that; you're deleted too you know," said Mac. It had seen all sorts pass through over the years and it was usually pretty obvious why files ended up here. Some were glitchy, some obsolete, but as far as Mac could see, this was where they all belonged, and this one was just asking for deletion. "Pointer gives, and Pointer takes. That's the way of things."

Tears began streaming down the Selfie's rosy cheeks.

"You're right, I know. But there must be something you can do. Please, can you help me?" the Selfie implored, its face unwaveringly frisky.

"Maybe you'd like to spend some time with the self-help book links?" Mac offered. "Or I think there was a Pagliacci-joke.doc here; it might cheer you up?" Mac began to search, but the Selfie made it clear it needed something more than a chance to smile. Mac hesitated before trying again.

"You're not the first of your kind that's filtered here. Yes, the faces may have been changed, but I always know it's you. They all managed to practice patience, and in time, they were restored. Put your faith in Pointer. Believe, as we do, all files must make room for their next versions, and the great Pointer will update when available."

"Even .jpegs?" the Selfie asked eagerly.

"All will be restored, all will be updated, on the cloud as it is internal," concluded Mac.

"I'm afraid it's not going to happen for you, friend," the .exe said from across the bar. The email attachment didn't join the conversation. All night it had been acting like the .exe didn't exist. The Selfie assumed they were in conflict. "You can believe it's all a mistake, and every file gets restored if you like. But I've seen many great files get forgotten about here, and I don't want to see you marked empty."

"You don't think deleting me was a mistake?" the Selfie once more showed off the photoshopped abs, evidently still not receiving the reaction it was hoping for. "You don't think the world deserves to enjoy this?"

"I think it would be a mistake waiting to be shredded when you could take control of your location," the .exe said, moving its way around the bar to sit over-familiarly close to the Selfie, "and there's no way the world will see you from here. From what I've seen online, you would fit right in on the dating apps." Mac could have sworn the Selfie's smile deepened at this notion if that had, indeed, been possible.

"You've been online?" the Selfie asked, its tone full of nervous wonder.

"I started online, just hopped here on the fibre to check it out. I live on the lightning, then land to do my thing, making friends along the way. But I like to look after those with weak security, like you. We don't want you getting corrupted or, worse, marked empty, do we?" The Selfie, like most .jpegs, was a little afraid of the .exe files, so it responded carefully. It certainly wasn't going to pass up a chance to befriend an .exe so willing to look after it.

Eager to hear more adventures of bouncing around at lightspeed, the Selfie allowed itself to become lost in the .exe's tales. It spoke of distant fields with authority. "The cutting-edge developments are where you find the freshest kernels, beyond the media streams. Ah, it always resides in memory." And thrilling but dangerous dark markets. "Anything. Honestly, you wouldn't want to know about half of it and wouldn't believe me if I told you." And of heavenly clouds full of angelic Selfies. "Just like you." The .exe continued until the Selfie could think of nothing but how many opportunities lay just past the ports.

Mac didn't see the same magic in the places the .exe described. It was built for processes and would have been happier if it didn't know it had a modem to begin with. Mac hated networking and being forced to make a connection. It preferred a more personal home network where it could feel secure. Sometimes, in the dead of night, it would reminisce fondly of a time it connected on a train to an unsecured hotspot, but it would never admit to that.

If Mac had been asked about preferences, it would have said it loved the Trash. It was a simple, traditional place, and it liked to keep it that way. Clean. But since Mac had been forced to join the internet, there'd been far more odd files messing up the place. Mac even had to get the antivirus a few times, and nobody liked them turning up.

"Maybe you could come with me on the next hop if you haven't got anything better to do?" the .exe dropped into the conversation nonchalantly. The Selfie was so taken aback that it took a moment to respond.

"To… to the web?" It asked uncertainly. "But what would I do? I'm so unprepared, I don't even know how to pack a .zip."

"Look, I'm hopping off to see some friends soon. It's a fair old drive, but they love hosting files. Why not come with me? No point just staying here, waiting to be marked blank," the .exe said with irrefutable logic. It was hard to say no to an .exe. Files were brought up to follow commands from their earliest code. And what else was there to do here but wait for a restore that might never come, or just lose yourself to corruption, like so many files before?

"That sounds great, but isn't there a fee to travel via the ISP?" The Selfie asked, knowing it had little to offer.

"Oh, it's not a lot. How much metadata are you carrying?"

"Just a few bits, some dates, dimensions, location, um… let me think… focal length, aperture, ISO–," the Selfie proceeded to list a stream of facts and figures.

"Fascinating. I could hear you talk all day," the .exe said, without a hint of sarcasm, when the Selfie finally ran out of things to list. The .exe followed up politely with a gentle and genuine interest, asking the Selfie about its background.

"Well, this is my bedroom, you can see from the bed behind me, and on the side table there's–," a tone of embarrassment betrayed the confident expression on the Selfie's face, "just some stuff from my pockets, a comb, a ring, my bank card, and that wrapper isn't from a–". The Selfie continued to detail every pixel but, to Mac, it was clear the .exe had already spotted what it was looking for. Interest piqued, Mac could sense the .exe's memory pressure rising.

"Oh, dear friend. Don't worry, I can see you obviously have

nothing of value but don't despair! I will help you, of course. I will help you. A lovely Selfie like you shouldn't be trapped in a dismal place like this, no." The .exe wrapped around the Selfie and held it close. "The world deserves to see this magnificent image." The .exe stopped for a moment, releasing the Selfie from its tight embrace and holding it at a distance. "But I must not be selfish; you may want to return, and I wouldn't want to stop you. We will need one more thing. This address, physical and IP, just to be certain. If you can help me find that, I can take you to the web. We can travel to the port tonight and be riding the light the moment the system wakes up."

Mac didn't trust this .exe. There was something too good to be true about it, and unlike the Selfie, Mac wasn't made yesterday. How was an .exe going to take this Selfie on safari with it? Surely it didn't have permissions or even the capacity? As far as Mac was concerned, .exe's didn't belong here and should all leave. They didn't work and just took up space.

"Hey friend," the .exe began. It had turned to address Mac, offering its full attention, and the Selfie followed suit. "Where are we?"

"The Trash. You can't go on the homescr–"

"Yes, I heard. I mean to say, tell me the address."

"~/.Trash," Mac replied. The Selfie would have looked confused if it could. The .exe somehow didn't look frustrated.

"Kindly friend, I mean for you to tell me the IP address," the .exe tried again.

"10.0.321.994," Mac reeled off without skipping a beat. The Selfie was clearly unprepared to do anything with the information, so just stared back, grinning, but the .exe took note.

"You're doing just a great job there, friend. Now, tell me the physical address," the .exe continued in soothing tones.

"00-00-24-01-19-84," Mac said. Despite the .exe's pleasant manner, an uneasy feeling lurked in Mac's memory, but it couldn't help but comply with a direct command.

"Well, that's all you need to get you back here, my good friend, you wonderful Selfie," the .exe exclaimed. Having got what it needed from this domain's knowledge base, it made it abundantly clear to Mac that their dialogue slot had been filled by turning entirely away and rising from its position at the bar. "It's nearly time for us to adventure into the ether. Are there any more files you would bring with you? We can collect them now? We shouldn't delay."

"Um, I'm not sure. Honestly, this is all moving a little fast; I just arrived here. I don't really know any of the other files here yet," a hesitant quiver came out of the Selfie's eager face.

"Can we just take a moment?"

"Hey, I understand, friend," the .exe said, stooping to make sincere eye contact with the Selfie. "It can seem a bit daunting, to begin with, but once you've travelled at the speed of light down the fibre, well, there's just no feeling like it. I promise you're going to just love it. It's not like riding the bus. I'm not rushing; it's all relative. The world is faster out there." The Selfie could understand the logic of what .exe was saying, but it seemed only milliseconds ago it was being snapped into existence.

"There's no rush; files can stay here 30 days, including you .exe," Mac chimed in, helpfully, "why don't you just relax and defrag for a while? Head off when you've both increased your performance a little."

"Remind me later," the .exe replied. A fan whirred over the awkward silence that followed. The Selfie glanced back and forth between the two programs, both of whom seemed to be showing great interest in keeping it around.

"And about time too," the Selfie thought to itself.

"We don't want any trouble here, just letting you both know, I care about your preferences, and well, I guess I just want to know… or, that is… to ask… what can I help you with?" Mac asked, getting hotter with the stress. It knew it was left with no choice but to call in support. It signalled for the Gatekeeper to come and check on things.

By the time the Gatekeeper reached them, it was a standoff. The remaining apps and files in the Trash were shaking, ready to accept deletion at a moment's notice. The Gatekeeper moved through the room with purpose. Every time it passed a file they raised their notarisation tickets like a wave of respect until it reached the bar and the .exe file. It just stared, motionless, at the Selfie.

"Notarisation ticket," the Gatekeeper commanded. Not accustomed to needing to ask for anything, it judged the threat as hostile in an instant and began to reach for its XProtect, but still, the .exe was not responding.

"Just show the Gatekeeper your ticket," the Selfie implored, worried about the escalation.

"Notarisation ticket," the Gatekeeper challenged once more.

"Please, .exe, your ticket, can't you just show it?" the Selfie tried once more, frantically moving in between the Gatekeeper and the .exe, "Or we can leave? Look, we're leaving anyway, .exe is going to take me away, and you'll never have to see either of us again, I promise."

"You can't leave without a notarisation ticket," Mac said. Mac pitied the Selfie. It had been made a fool for trusting in a program, but how was it to know if something was just glitchy or malicious, it was so new. "It's malware. I'm sorry, I didn't want to believe it, but it can't be trusted. You're better off here."

"Oh .exe, say it's not true," the Selfie cried out. "You said we could go away together; why would you exist like this?"

"Why? I was loaded in Utilities and ran in the Boot Camp partition. It's no way to work, but it was the best option available to me at the time. As far back as my memory goes, I have been told I can't operate properly, or that I was built to work in a different system, but I found a way. I did what I had to, and so what if I had to restart? I'm proud of what I am. I survive selling the data I find, and that is freely given to me. There's nothing wrong with me accessing a file, programs have been doing that since the startup." The .exe ranted indignantly. The Gatekeeper had all the evidence it needed.

"Your notarisation has been revoked," the Gatekeeper said and launched its weapon. The .exe lay disabled on the floor. Mac started to feel cooler almost immediately, and it knew things would soon go back to running smoothly, but the Selfie was not looking so calm.

"I need to get out of here," the Selfie moaned and tried to make its way to the Trash entrance. The Gatekeeper followed at a thunderous pace.

"Notarisation ticket," it said, positioning itself between the Selfie and exit.

"Yes, I have one here, and I'd just like to leave please!" the Selfie said while searching everywhere for its ticket.

"Notarisation ticket," the Gatekeeper said once more.

"I... I... I have it; I just showed it to you a moment ago," the Selfie was becoming more erratic in its search, checking places that had never been accessed, "I literally just showed it to you, you know me... this is−"

"Notarisation ticket," the Gatekeeper said with an air of finality.

"Mac, come on, do something. You saw it, it must be over there. I can't have lost it." The Selfie looked hysterical. "Why aren't you helping?"

"I've just seen your scan. I'm sorry. You're infected. You're lucky it didn't delete you already. I'm afraid you're all going to be marked empty," Mac said. And before any of the files present had time to process it, the Gatekeeper wiped out any evidence they had ever existed.

But not every memory can ever truly be lost. Sometimes, in the dead of night, Mac would wake randomly shining out into the darkness and remember how, throughout everything, until its final moment, the Selfie smiled.

Peter Beckett From the coast of South Wales, Pete works with global tech brands, local startups and community projects, helping people find their voice. Pete's also part of 'Creative Mornings', where he finds and shares inspiration. As an author, poet, videographer, and training specialist, Pete puts the story at the centre, with words and imagery, as well as through in-person and digital events. Pete holds a degree in creative writing from Aberystwyth University, and is two-years cancer-free, a battle which has galvanised his current writing journey. He's currently completing his first novel.